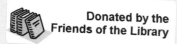

ROBOT WARS

SIGMUND BROUWER

BOOK FIVE

FINAL
BATTLE

TYNDALE HOUSE PUBLISHERS, INC.
CAROL STREAM, ILLINOIS

You can contact Sigmund Brouwer through his website at www.coolreading.com or www.whomadethemoon.com.

Visit Tyndale's website for kids at www.tyndale.com/kids.

TYNDALE and Tyndale's quill logo are registered trademarks of Tyndale House Publishers, Inc.

Final Battle

Previously published as Mars Diaries *Mission 9: Manchurian Sector* and Mars Diaries *Mission 10: Last Stand* under ISBNs 0-8423-5633-9 and 0-8423-5634-7.

Final Battle first published in 2009.

Designed by Mark Anthony Lane II

This novel is a work of fiction. Names, characters, places, and incidents either are the product of the author's imagination or are used fictitiously. Any resemblance to actual events, locales, organizations, or persons living or dead is entirely coincidental and beyond the intent of either the author or the publisher.

For manufacturing information regarding this product, please call 1-800-323-9400.

Library of Congress Cataloging-in-Publication Data

Brouwer, Sigmund, date.
   Final battle / Sigmund Brouwer.
     p. cm. — (Robot wars ; bk. 5)
   Previously published separately in 2002 as Mars Diaries, Mission 9: Manchurian Sector; and Mars Diaries, Mission 10: Last Stand.
   Summary: In the first of two adventures set in 2040, fourteen-year-old, wheelchair-bound, virtual reality specialist, Tyce Sanders is forced to reveal his special talents in order to avert a nuclear reactor explosion, and in the second, Tyce and his friend Ashley must find a way to stop a dreaded Manchurian fleet from overtaking the Earth.
   ISBN 978-1-4143-2313-8 (softcover)
   [1. Science fiction. 2. Robots—Fiction. 3. People with disabilities—Fiction. 4. Virtual reality—Fiction. 5. Christian life—Fiction.] I. Brouwer, Sigmund, date. Mars diaries. Mission 9. Manchurian sector. II. Brouwer, Sigmund, date. Mars diaries. Mission 10. Last stand. III. Title.
   PZ7.B79984Fin 2009
   [Fic]—dc22   2009016772

Printed in the United States of America

17 16 15 14 13 12 11
8   7   6   5   4   3   2

THIS SERIES IS DEDICATED
IN MEMORY OF MARTYN GODFREY.

Martyn, you wrote books that reached all of us kids at heart. You wrote them because you really cared. We all miss you.

FROM THE AUTHOR

We live in amazing times! When I first began writing these
Mars journals, not even 40 years after our technology allowed
us to put men on the moon, the concept of robot control was
strictly something I daydreamed about when readers first
met Tyce. Since then, science fiction has been science fact.
Successful experiments have now been performed on monkeys
who are able to use their brains to control robots halfway
around the world!

Suddenly it's not so far-fetched to believe that these
adventures could happen for Tyce. Or for you. Or for your
children.

With that in mind, I hope you enjoy stepping into a
future that could really happen. . . .

Sigmund Brouwer

JOURNAL
ONE

CHAPTER 1

Radiation blast!

Behind me, three doors—each three feet thick and made of steel-encased concrete—were already open to the outer world. Ahead was the final door protecting the inner core of the nuclear reactor at the power plant. It was the final barrier between me and the intense heat and radiation about to blast me when a computer signal triggered it to open like the ones behind me.

Had my body been there in my wheelchair, the heat would have made puddles of my skin and flesh, reducing me to bones and skull. Just as deadly were the radiation waves coming from the reactor's uranium core, only a half hour away from a final and catastrophic meltdown.

Fortunately I had not approached in my wheelchair but

through a robot body that had rolled under my control through the first three doorways toward that last door. In theory, my task was simple. Pull the rod of uranium from the sheath that fueled the reactor, shutting it down. But I had to do it fast—all before the entire reactor exploded in a mushroom cloud with five times the power of any nuclear bomb.

And all because of bad hamburgers.

Ten hours earlier, a bizarre chain of events had begun the meltdown. First, one of the power plant transformers had been struck by lightning, triggering three massive, key surge protectors. This in itself would have done no serious damage. After all, engineers had installed the surge protectors for something exactly like this. What they hadn't planned on was a second lightning bolt hitting the same transformer within the next 10 seconds. Millions of volts had overwhelmed the power plant's internal systems, crashing half the computers and scrambling the other half.

Even so, the problem should have ended there. At any given time, three technicians were on shift to monitor the system. In an emergency such as this one, only two of the technicians are needed to hit twin fail-safe controls on each side of the massive monitoring panel, and a computer would begin shutting down the nuclear reactor.

Shutting down the nuclear reactor wasn't something

you wanted to do every day, though. The city of Los Angeles, California, would lose the electrical power supplied by this nuclear plant. And it would take 10 days to complete the shutdown and then get the nuclear core up and running again to restore power to the city.

But now, compared to the alternative, 10 days of blackout was a cheap price to pay. Because if the nuclear core exploded, its shock waves would kill every person within 30 miles. And with the wind blowing as it was, deadly radioactive dust would cover everyone else for another 20 miles beyond to the west.

Which meant all of Los Angeles. With the freeways jammed to a standstill by people trying to flee in panic.

In short, on any other day the one-in-a-hundred-million chance of a second lightning bolt would have led to an immediate and inconvenient shutdown.

Except for those uncooked hamburgers.

All three night-shift technicians had shared some takeout burgers as they carpooled to work that evening. And all three had gotten violently sick halfway through their shift. With one technician in the bathroom, the other two had stayed, doubled over in agony in front of the controls. That's why they had missed the first warning lights on the control board. Backup sirens had alerted them 30 seconds later. Sick or not, they knew what needed to be done: count down so that each could hit his own shutdown button. Both buttons had to be pressed at exactly the same time to begin the shutdown.

But the retching and dizziness caused by the bad hamburgers had proved to be too much strain for the older of the two remaining technicians. He had fainted and fallen backward as he reached for the shutdown control.

How did I know this? All of it was well documented on the video loop that monitored the control room. With one technician in the bathroom and one unconscious on the control-room floor, the sole technician remaining at the control board was helpless. He could reach only one shutdown control at a time. When the technician returned from the bathroom two minutes later, the nuclear core was out of control.

That's why I'd been sent. I'm Tyce Sanders. Fourteen years old and very new to Earth. I was supposed to be on an urgent secret mission to the Moon: locating a missing pod of kids like me, who could control robots using their own brain waves. Instead, because of this Earth emergency, high-ranking Combat Force military officials had flown me in early this morning, 04.02.2040, by supersonic jet from New York City, where I was supposed to meet with the military higher-ups, to an L.A. military base, with my robot beside me.

As if this wasn't enough stress, just a day earlier my friend Ashley and I had nearly died. We and our robots helped stop a terrorist plot that would have killed all the supreme governors of the World United Federation—what used to be called the *United Nations* when my dad was a kid. Ashley was in the desert mountains of Arizona, helping with the other robot-control kids who had just been rescued.

And I'd been sent here to California. With the thunderstorm that had begun the blowout long gone, the weather had been perfect for flying. As the jet circled the Los Angeles basin on its approach to the Combat Force base, the military division of the World United Federation, I had a clear view of the almost endless city sprawl and the autopilot vehicles that plugged the highways.

The city was in a valley, guarded by the jagged edges of the green-brown mountains against blue sky. I took in the view with awe, since the planet I'd lived on all my life—Mars—looked so different. There the mountains are red, and during the day, the sun is blue against a butterscotch-colored sky.

Nuclear plant officials had spoken to me by videophone almost the entire flight, explaining the situation and trying to prepare me for my task. Time was running short, so they couldn't afford to give me instructions on my arrival.

Once the jet touched ground in L.A., it had taken another two hours for the nuclear experts to coach me through the training session. Or, more precisely, for me to run the robot through its training session. Again and again and again. I would have only one chance. If I made the slightest mistake, I might actually trigger an earlier meltdown.

Which would kill me just as surely as everyone else in

the meltdown zone. Because I was only a mile away from the nuclear plant, controlling the robot by remote from my wheelchair.

Now the fourth and final door began to open, and I focused all my attention on the task ahead.

I'd already shut down the robot's heat sensors. Although the titanium skin of my robot was far more durable than my own skin, I didn't want my brain to panic, telling me my body was in a furnace.

A vertical bar of intense white heat widened as the door opened more.

I directed my robot to reach up with its right arm and flip down a protective shield of black glass to reduce the glare. Otherwise, with the light rays reaching my brain through the robot's video lenses, it would be like staring into the sun. I was already in a wheelchair. I didn't want to become blind too.

Mentally I braced myself to rush the robot forward. Even with the robot's asbestos cape for protection, the technicians figured it would not last for more than 30 seconds against the heat.

So that's all I had. Thirty seconds.

If the robot even continued to function once the radiation hit.

The technicians' biggest fear was that the intense radiation would interfere with the robot's computer drive, which received signals from a transmitter that was directly linked to a plug in my spinal column, and from there to my brain. I shared that fear. If the robot failed to operate, the nuclear plant would blow. And no one could guess if the radiation interference might scramble the transmissions enough to affect my brain. You see, if a robot is zapped with an electrical current, the controller is knocked unconscious at a minimum or perhaps even killed. As for radiation interference . . . well, that could be far more deadly.

But with the door three-quarters open, I had no time to worry anymore.

I could see a huge glow through the black glass of my protective shield. Somewhere in the center of it was a rod the length and width of a person's arm. I had to pull it loose before the robot lost its function.

The door stopped opening, then sagged slightly. Had the heat melted its hinges?

I didn't hesitate. My robot was nearly six feet tall, 150 pounds, and incredibly strong. I surged forward, smashing into the door.

Pain instantly shot through me in my wheelchair. The virtual-reality program that enables me to control a robot is so real, it felt like my left arm had broken. I tried to get the robot's left arm to wave. It wouldn't. I'd demolished it against the door.

But the door was open, and I was through.

At the center of the huge glow filling the room was a rod-shaped whiteness almost unbearable to see, even with the black glass that protected the robot's video lenses.

I had to act quickly. The robot already felt sluggish.

I commanded it forward. It lurched, stopped, then lurched again.

Radiation interference!

I'd spent 10 seconds, and the robot was only halfway there. With all my concentration, I commanded it to continue. Then . . . *clunk.*

It had hit the far end. The core was within reach. All I had to do was somehow get the robot's right arm up and . . .

Another 10 seconds.

The robot's arm began to glow. Would it last long enough to . . . ?

The robot's titanium hand closed on the end of the core rod and fused instantly. That didn't matter. We'd expected that.

What I had to do now was roll backward and . . .

A sluggishness hit my own brain. Like black glue oozing into my skull.

Come on! I shouted mentally. *Come on! Think!*

In my mind, it felt like I was falling backward. Backward. Backward.

And then the black glue froze all of my thoughts.

Silence squeezed my consciousness into total darkness.

CHAPTER 2

I was startled awake with the feeling of something damp on
my forehead.

Opening my eyes, I saw a nurse, probably a little older
than my mother. She wiped my forehead with a cool, damp
sponge.

Then I remembered. I was in a hospital somewhere in
L.A. I'd woken up late last night as doctors poked and prodded
at my body. They had dryly informed me that I was a hero. As
my robot had fallen backward, it had pulled the core of uranium far enough out of the sheath to prevent the final stage of
uncontrolled nuclear fission. I'd grimaced. With my killer headache, I hadn't felt like a hero. Just like a kid who missed his
home. Which for me, of course, was Mars. Then the doctors had
given me a painkiller for my headache and let me sleep again.

I guess I'd slept all the way through 'til the next day.

"Good to see you awake," the nurse said. "You gave everybody a scare."

Right now, she was scaring me. The only thing normal about her was the light green nurse's uniform. Her platinum-colored hair was so shiny and piled so high, I knew it had to be a wig. Especially because it wasn't a natural color for a woman with skin darker than chocolate. Her lips were smeared with purple lipstick, and I was ready to choke on the smell of her heavy perfume.

She smiled, showing gleaming white teeth that were surprisingly straight and even. Like she'd spent a lot of money on those teeth but cheaped out on the horrible wig. "Of course, that nuclear plant gave everyone a scare too. What was it like in there?"

"It all happened so fast," I answered, trying not to stare at her bad makeup. I'd never gone trick-or-treating—we never celebrated Halloween on Mars—but I knew about it and wondered if somehow I'd been in a coma so long that it was now October 31.

"Well, I think you were brave," she replied kindly. "Even if you didn't have to go in yourself. That robot . . . you controlled it, right?"

I nodded, wondering if my head would hurt like it had last night. It didn't. I relaxed a little. Weird thing was, something about this nurse looked familiar. Like maybe I'd seen her in a movie from one of the DVD-gigaroms I'd watched growing up on Mars.

I grinned at my strange thoughts. It must be the shock I'd had. I was imagining things. A woman in a wig like this would never be on camera.

"I control the robot with my brain," I answered. No matter how she looked, I reminded myself she was trying to be nice. "Like it's a virtual-reality game. Except I move a real robot, not something in a computer program."

"Wow." A big, encouraging smile again. "Your parents must be proud of you."

I did my best to hide a frown. *My parents.* Mom was a plant biologist on Mars, millions and millions of miles away. I missed her badly, along with my friend Rawling, who'd taught me how to control robots when I was a little kid. I wondered what they were doing right now, in another part of the solar system.

As for my dad, Chase Sanders, I didn't even know where he was. Dad was a space pilot. He'd taken the first shuttle to Mars over 15 years earlier. On that eight-month trip he'd met my mom, Kristy Wallace, who was also part of the first expedition of scientists to set up a colony on Mars. They had gotten married as soon as they reached the red planet, and I'd been born almost a year later.

That's why I'd never seen Earth until I came back with Dad on his most recent shuttle from Mars. But something

had gone wrong. Dad, Ashley, and I had been arrested almost
as soon as we reached the Earth's orbit. We'd been taken
to a military prison in the swamps of Florida. But because
Dad held some old guy hostage—I found out later he was the
supreme governor of the World United Federation—Ashley
and I had been able to escape the Combat Force prison. Dad
had told us to go ahead with our mission and that we had a
six-day countdown to find the pod of kids Ashley had been a
part of. Otherwise it would be too late. And then sometime
in the middle of our mission, we'd heard that Dad had disappeared. No one had heard from him since. Until the nuclear
plant thing, he had been my biggest worry. And now—with
this nurse's question as a reminder—my worry returned.

"I'll bet you don't know what your father might think,"
she said, lowering her voice and leaning forward to whisper,
"since you haven't spoken to him since you escaped prison,
have you? And you know that he's disappeared. . . ."

Her words had the same effect as if she'd jammed an
electric prod into my chest. Only the top people in the Combat
Force of the World United Federation knew about my dad. Or
that he'd been put in prison as soon as he'd arrived on Earth.

"How do you know about my—?"

She put one finger over her lips.

I stopped speaking.

She leaned over farther and put her face up to my ear.
She spoke softly as I held my breath, trying not to gag on the

smell of her perfume. "There's a reason I'm whispering. You need to assume that electronic devices are set up to listen to whatever you say. To anybody at any time. Not everyone in the Combat Force is on your side."

I pushed my face close to hers. Loose hairs from the platinum wig tickled my nose. "My father?" I asked in a whisper to match hers. "If you know where he is—"

"What I know," she whispered back, "is that the World United Federation won't be able to keep your robot-control abilities secret from the world any longer. Not after the nuclear plant."

"My dad. What do you know about—?"

"Even the Terratakers within the Combat Force realized they couldn't put all those millions of lives at risk to protect the secret of this new technology. A hundred lives, sure. A thousand. Maybe even 10,000 lives. But not the entire Los Angeles basin. When it came down to deciding between keeping you under wraps or stopping the blowout, they made the right choice. But that means you are now in great danger."

As if that was news. For the past nine months somebody had been trying to kill me. And I knew the rebel faction, the Terratakers, was involved, because of Dr. Jordan, who had tried to kill Dad, Ashley, and me by sending our shuttle into the sun. The Terratakers had spies everywhere, and they fought hard against the World United Federation. Unlike the Federation, which worked to find solutions for Earth's growing population, such as making planets like Mars suitable for humans, the Terratakers were a terrorist organization that worked against the colonization of Mars. Instead they claimed the Earth's population should be reduced. Fewer babies should be born. And when humans had outlived their usefulness, they should be put to sleep.

What the Terratakers believed was pretty scary. Because if you followed what they believed, it meant I wouldn't be alive. To them, someone in a wheelchair with useless legs isn't worth enough to use valuable water and food.

"My dad," I insisted. It seemed weird enough to be a dream. All of our conversation was in a low whisper. Although this woman had on enough makeup to be a clown, I had no choice but to take her seriously because of what she knew.

"Remember, the Combat Force has too many Terrataker traitors inside it. That's why they were almost able to storm the Summit of Governors."

The Summit of Governors! Where all the world leaders gather each year to deal with international problems.

She straightened and stared at me to see if I understood what it meant that she knew about the summit. The surprise on my face must have shown.

"I know," she whispered, leaning forward again. "The attempt on the governors' lives was supposed to be a secret too. You can't imagine the steps the Combat Force took to bury that. And the danger of robot soldiers controlled by an army of kids. Except now they'll decide to show you off to the world. And put you at great risk."

"You can't know this!" The Summit of Governors in New York City had been meeting to talk about whether or not to continue the funding of the Mars Project: the colonization of Mars. And it had come within 30 seconds of ending with all the leaders being shot by robot soldiers controlled by the Terrataker faction. Yet the world didn't know about it. The newspapers had reported the commotion around the summit as a Hollywood stunt for the promotion of an upcoming movie. To the public, it was as if nothing had happened.

"I do know this. Which should tell you that all the rest of what I'm telling you is true."

"My dad. What about—?"

Someone knocked at the door. It was another nurse. Much younger, with spiked red hair and a nose ring.

"Hello?" The red-haired nurse seemed confused. "This is my room on the duty chart," she said to the older nurse at my bed. "I didn't know another shift had started."

The nurse in front of me straightened out the sheets of my bed. "Obviously there's been a mistake. Why don't you check at the front desk?"

"But—"

"Don't mess with me, girl. Just go to the front desk and make sure you got that duty chart right," the platinum blonde nurse said. She'd been talking to me in a normal voice.

Talking to this new nurse, suddenly her voice was high and whiny to match the way she looked. Who *was* this woman with the bad lipstick?

"Okay," the red-haired nurse said after a second. "I'll be right back." We could hear the soft sound of her shoes padding down the hallway.

"Time to go," my perfumed nurse said. Her voice was normal again. "And remember what I said."

I wanted to know about my dad. "Don't go," I pleaded.

We heard the distant sounds of shoes in the hallway. Headed our way from the front desk.

"Can't stay," she said simply. And with that, she was gone. Whoever she was.

Gone. With whatever else she knew.

CHAPTER 3

A tall, broad-shouldered man nodded at me and sat down beside my bed. A man in Combat Force uniform. General Jeb McNamee, known as Cannon, had a face ugly enough to scare little children—a square face, bent nose, and shaved head. He was the kind of man you wanted on your side.

Listening devices, the mysterious nurse had said.

If they were here, it wasn't because of this military man. After all, he had sent Nate, who'd been part of Cannon's elite unit in the Combat Force called the EAGLES. And Nate had helped Ashley and me flee the Florida Everglades. Then Cannon himself had helped us find and rescue the pod of robot kids in Arizona. But was the nurse in the hospital right? Could no one be trusted? Did the infiltration of the Terratakers extend even to people like Cannon, who seemed to be on my side?

"Good to see you bright-eyed," the general said in his gruff voice. "For a while there, I thought we'd be giving you a 21-gun salute."

"Twenty-one-gun salute?"

"A military tradition. An honor at funeral ceremonies. Twenty-one shots fired in the air. The total of one and seven and seven and six. It started as an American tradition, and now all the Federation military in the world follow the custom." He squinted at me to see if I would figure it out.

"One seven seven six," I repeated slowly. "Seventeen seventy-six." I got it. And grinned. "The year the United States declared its independence from England."

"Yes, sir," Cannon said. "Glad to see your brains are still intact." He patted my shoulder.

Terrataker traitors are everywhere in the military. But I can trust Cannon, I told myself. Yet I didn't like the little bit of doubt in the back of my mind.

Yes, I decided, I would trust Cannon. Chad, his own son, was still among some of the missing kids who had been kidnapped at a young age to be operated on for robot control. And, in searching for his son, Cannon had been the main person responsible for stopping the Summit of Governors assassination attempt. He'd helped save my life.

Surely he couldn't be one of the high-level traitors inside the World United Federation's Combat Force.

I wanted to tell Cannon about the strange woman. But if there were listening devices . . .

My dad was out there. Somewhere, needing help.

To be on the safe side, I decided to wait to tell Cannon about the nurse with the strange message. Or about the red-haired nurse coming back and saying no other nurse was supposed to be on duty. That had convinced me the strange message hadn't come from a real nurse but someone dressed up to look like a nurse. Who was she, really? That question burned inside me.

"Tyce, I've got some exciting news," Cannon said.

"My father?"

"Not yet. But don't worry. We have the resources of the entire Combat Force at our disposal," he assured me. Then he continued. "It's about Mars. Now it looks like we can push the colonization schedule ahead by 50 years."

"Fifty years! That might save millions of lives!"

Mom and Rawling would love to hear this, if they hadn't already. After all, they'd been working for that very thing for the past 15 years. The establishment of a dome under which people could live on Mars was only Phase 1 of a long-term plan. Phase 2, which the Mars colony was now in, was to grow plant hybrids outside the dome so that more oxygen could be added to the atmosphere. The long-range plan—which could take over 100 years—was to make the entire planet a place for humans to live outside the dome.

People on Earth desperately needed the room. Already the planet had too few resources for the many people on it. If Mars could be made a new colony, then Earth could start shipping people there to live. If not, new wars might begin, and millions and millions of people would die from war or starvation or disease. Even now countries verged on war because of the diminishing amount of resources.

"Fifty years," Cannon repeated. "The irony is that we'll be using a method that would never be welcome on Earth: pollution. At least, pollution in the form of carbon dioxide."

Cannon explained. On Earth, too much carbon dioxide caused the greenhouse effect. Light from the sun entered Earth's atmosphere and was not able to bounce back into outer space. Carbon dioxide trapped heat. That was not good on Earth, but on the cold planet of Mars, it would be great. Yes, most of the atmosphere of Mars already consisted of carbon dioxide. But there wasn't enough atmosphere. If billions of tons more could be added, then finally Mars would start absorbing heat.

"Scientists have had the plans in place for building the generators and even for shipping them in pieces to Mars. But until now it was impossible to assemble them except at too great a cost."

"Carbon-dioxide generators." I imagined clouds of white gas mushrooming and vanishing on the barren surface of the red planet. Mushrooming and mushrooming for years and years. And plants could live in the thickening atmosphere, breathing in carbon dioxide and releasing oxygen that wouldn't drift into outer space because finally there would be enough atmosphere to hold it in.

"What's truly made this possible is you," Cannon continued. "You in particular. And all the others with robot-control abilities. Let me explain."

Again, I listened.

"Because there are enough kids like you, who can volunteer to assemble the generators easily on the surface of Mars. Technicians need bulky space suits, which can rip far too easily. Kids safe inside the dome, though, can handle robots outside the dome. Robots that don't need air or water. Those robots can work 100 times faster than humans. We can get the generators up and running in a matter of months. Kids who volunteer will be amply repaid by the government. The important thing now is that Tyce Sanders gets support from all Earth countries to undertake this next phase."

"Me?" I asked, stunned.

"This will sound cold, Tyce. But you are the perfect public relations opportunity. Many of the highest-ranking Combat Force officials were determined to keep robot control a secret as long as possible. They were afraid the world would see only the negatives. Especially if they found out about the soldier robots. But now they can see the positives. We are going to introduce you to the world as the hero you are. And people won't be afraid of robot control."

It was strange. Throughout my life I'd always thought of myself as just a kid. A kid in a wheelchair. And now the very thing that had put me in a wheelchair—the surgery that had inserted a plug in my spine so that I could control robots—made me a hero. Weird. Well, I guess it was true what Mom always said: God does use our disabilities for good.

The words of the mysterious nurse came back to me. *"The attempt on the governors' lives was supposed to be a secret too. You can't imagine the steps the Combat Force took to bury that. And the danger of robot soldiers controlled by an army of kids. Except now they'll decide to show you off to the world. And put you at great risk."*

What she predicted was happening right now.

It was almost as if Cannon had read my suspicious thoughts—thoughts I didn't want to have about him.

"I apologize," he said. "In a way, we are using you. I hope you'll allow that, however. We desperately need approval of robot control in public-opinion polls all over the world. With that approval, politicians will support the next phase of Mars development. Without it, opposition will ground us. And the Terratakers will win."

"I'll do what I can to help," I finally said.

"Thank you." He spoke with dignity. "We'll immediately set up a media conference at the World United Federation Center in New York. And after that . . ."

I waited. I didn't like the concern etched into Cannon's face.

". . . I think you'll need to go to the Moon. There's that last pod of missing kids. They need our help."

"Yes, sir," I agreed.

"There's more. Lots more."

"Sir?"

He stood. "The doctors tell me you're ready to go. Let me explain the rest of it on the way back to New York."

CHAPTER 4

"Tantalum."

"I beg your pardon, sir?"

It had taken barely a half hour to get in the air. A helicopter had flown us from the hospital to the runway, where a jet waited. So Cannon and I now sat in a military jet, traveling 30,000 feet above the ground, headed back to New York at 600 miles an hour. The shades on the windows had been pulled down, and a projector was set up between us.

"It's a rare metal," he answered from the darkness. "So rare and precious that it shouldn't be a surprise that kids like you have been put into slavery to mine it."

Slavery. Kids like me. Able to control robots. But unlike me, unable to control anything else in their lives.

"Let me back up a second." He clicked a button on his

remote, and a photo of the Moon's surface appeared on a screen in front of us. At least I guessed it was the Moon. In the darkness beyond it was the familiar blue and white ball of Earth that I had watched so often from a telescope on Mars. In the foreground of the photo, beyond small craters of the gray soil, was a platform buggy—four wheels that support a deck, covered by a dome—about to enter a low, flat building.

"In its purest form, tantalum is a rare gray-white metal. Melting point at about 3,000 degrees Celsius and boiling point at well over 5,000 degrees Celsius. Pure tantalum is extremely flexible. It can be drawn into microscopically thin wires. At normal temperatures, it's almost impossible to corrode with any acid. Its chief use is in computer components."

"I think I understand," I said. The hum of the jet engines forced me to raise my voice. "Computers are everywhere, so if tantalum is rare . . ."

"Exactly. The more computers, the more it is needed. The more it is needed, the more it is worth. Right now, it has about 100 times the value of gold. Historically, it was mined in Africa and Canada. Those mines are basically depleted. But major deposits were recently discovered on the Moon. In the sector controlled by the Manchurians."

"The Manchurian Sector . . ." I knew some history. Manchuria was a province in China. Although the area itself had not expanded over the last 50 years, its political influence had gone far beyond China.

General Cannon clicked his remote again. A new photo flashed onto the screen. This one was not of the surface of the Moon. It was an interior shot—I guessed the inside of the building in the photo before. It was like a large warehouse. Lights hung from overhead. Men in space suits tended to a platform buggy. But in the background were . . .

Another click brought the background closer and into full focus.

Robots! Just like the one I controlled. I didn't have to say it. Cannon wouldn't be showing me this unless it meant the pod of missing kids was involved.

"Once again, let me back up," the general said. "You probably know enough about Earth politics to understand that each country within the World United Federation is independent."

"Yes," I said. "But the world population crisis forced the countries to work closer together and form an alliance. Just like different states within the United States work together. But the Terratakers wanted to make sure that didn't happen." I shivered slightly.

Cannon leaned toward me. "I want to let you in on a military reality and the war no one will admit is being fought," he said. "Publicly it's believed that the Terratakers consist of individuals from each country who believe in a cause. Much like the environmentalists of the previous century."

"It's not true?"

"No," the general grimly answered. I strained to hear over the noise of the jet. "When the World United Federation formed, there were two military superpowers that balanced each other—the United States and China. Late in the 20th century, the Russians fell by the wayside as their economy collapsed. As Russia fell, China stepped into the vacuum and began to dominate until it almost rivaled the United States. It was a peaceful rivalry, until the Manchurians came to power."

"A political base in China that defied their country's mandate of world trade," I said. "It divided China into pro- and anti-American rivalries. And then rebels within other countries across the world began to identify with the Manchurian movement. The World United Federation is not allowed to interfere with internal difficulties of any country. The Manchurians won a brief civil war within China and now call the shots there."

I grinned at Cannon's raised eyebrows. "Hey, home-schooling is a big deal on Mars. And I was the only student on the planet. So I had to learn everything."

Cannon grinned back, then got serious. "To both China and the U.S., the goals of the World United Federation are far too important to risk open war. Yet beneath the surface, the Americans are locked in battle against the Manchurian movement for dominance. It's like the Cold War that took place between the United States and Russia for 45 years after

World War II. We have our spies. They have theirs. And if the Terratakers succeed, it will shift the balance of power to the Manchurians."

"You're saying the Terratakers are backed by the Manchurians?"

"Exactly," Cannon said. "And all the other countries that would openly side with the Manchurians if they ever thought the Americans would be defeated in a world war."

"I think I understand," I said. "Publicly, all countries stay in line with the World United Federation because of the power of the United States. But the ones waiting for the slightest chance are working with the Manchurians. And now you're telling me the Manchurians and Terratakers . . ."

"The Manchurians didn't form the Terrataker political movement. But once it happened, the Manchurians took advantage of the terrorist organization. After all, they already shared some of the Terratakers' philosophy on population control: to limit the number of children a family could have. And they had openly supported the United States' Human Genome Project, which began in 1990."

"The Genome Project?" I asked, curious.

"It began as a way to identify genes and map human DNA, so that humans would know if they were carrying a genetic disease or not. But soon it was being used to identify and convict criminals and to test not-yet-born babies for genetic defects. Now scientists in the Terrataker camp are

arguing that everyone in the world should be routinely tested
and the results kept on file. It frightens me to think of how
they might use that information—to abort any babies with
genetic defects, for example." The general cleared his throat.
"Yet we can't openly accuse the Manchurians of supporting
the Terratakers. It would be too easy for them to deny it and
too easy for them to use those charges to swing world opinion
in their favor. But we know it's happening. For example, Luke
Daab and Dr. Jordan—"

"Terrataker agents! You mean they're not only running
this robot-control program, but with Manchurian help?"

"Yes," the general said calmly. "Without the money and
resources made available to them by a military superpower,
those two men wouldn't have been able to accomplish anything. Instead . . ."

General Cannon didn't have to say more about that.
Both men had come very close to killing me on Mars and on
the journey from Mars. Both men had engineered the assassination attempt at the Summit of Governors.

"Let me put it this way, Tyce. In the end, whoever controls
Mars will control the power on Earth." The general paused.

That was a pretty scary thought. With the Terratakers
in control, human life would become disposable. Like diapers. People like me with disabilities wouldn't be around. Old
people would be killed. Babies with genetic defects wouldn't
be allowed to be born.

My brain spun with the possibilities. The DNA you were born with would control whether you lived or died, your right to attend college, even what job you were allowed to have. . . . A doctor's simple test of your DNA could determine not only your life, but the quality and length of your life. But did other humans have the right to choose what was really in God's hands?

"Within the Federation," Cannon continued, "the United States government is working hard to keep the Mars Project a neutral one, governed by all countries. But the Terratakers want to have it all to themselves. It's a strange balancing act in public perception. On the surface the Terratakers seem passionately opposed to space exploration and expansion. But what they really oppose is Federation control of the planet. They want it for themselves. The Manchurians want it to publicly appear as if they support Federation control of Mars, but secretly they want it for themselves too. Because if they ever gain control of Mars and its resources, they will openly try to take over the Federation on Earth. And if that happens, the solar system will be theirs. That's why the Terratakers and Manchurians are so willing to work together. The Manchurians have structure and political control but must keep a respectable appearance. The Terratakers have a dirty reputation and are willing to do the dirty work, but they need the power and resources of the Manchurians."

I kept staring at the photo that showed robots beneath

a warehouse building on the Moon. "If the warehouse on the Moon is in the Manchurian Sector, it's protected, right?"

"According to Federation structure, yes. Countries have individual rights. On Earth, the Manchurian military can't enter the United States without permission. Nor can they enter our sector on the Moon. The same is true, of course, in reverse. Their sector has total immunity, which extends even to their orbit stations in space. It's a prime example of how the Manchurians are able to help the Terratakers."

General Cannon clicked again. The next photo showed an extreme close-up of a robot.

"Some time ago, a Federation agent managed to sneak in as a worker and send these photos by satellite. But we're guessing he was caught. At least we haven't heard from him since. At the time, we thought China had extremely sophisticated robots. But now, because of you, we know better. The only thing that makes sense is that the robots are controlled by human brains."

"So that's why you think the last pod of kids is on the Moon?" I thought of what I'd seen four days ago in Arizona for the first time. Kids trapped in huge jelly tubes, in 24-hour-a-day life support. Unable to move and hooked to computers under the control of Dr. Jordan.

"I can't answer that," Cannon said. "All we know for sure about the operation is what the public knows. Great quantities of tantalum are shipped from the Manchurian

Sector on the Moon to Earth. That means massive amounts of money are transferred to the Manchurian coalition, which in turn is able to finance more Terrataker action against the Federation. This money has also attracted other countries to unofficially back the Manchurians. We're talking far more than a China power base."

He scratched his head. "And the worst part is that we have no way of proving our theory: that those robots are controlled by the last pod of kids. We can't get into that warehouse. But if we could prove to the world what's happening, the Manchurians will lose most of their support."

He paused. "I believe my son is among those slaves. So what I'm about to ask is for more than the Federation. It's for me personally. Tyce, will you go into that warehouse in the Manchurian Sector and bring us back the proof we need to help those kids?"

CHAPTER 5

Pop! Pop! Pop!

Although the blinding light made no sound, my head hurt so badly it seemed like I could hear each flash from each camera. I'd only been back in New York for less than a day, and I hadn't been out of the hospital long enough.

Pop! Pop! Pop!

Cannon kept a hand on my shoulder, walking beside me as I rolled my wheelchair toward dozens of photographers gathered below the front of the enormous stage for the morning's press conference. Boom mikes hung in the air above them. Television cameras were mounted on each side.

"You're right," I told Cannon.

"Right?"

"When you said that they look like a—"

He squeezed my shoulder hard. "Not here. You never know what their recording equipment will pick up."

I'd been about to say they looked like a pack of hungry jackals. Because, of course, that had been the general's description in the back room five minutes earlier as we went over the news conference material.

"You ready?" the general asked in a low voice. "We can always turn back. Even now."

We neared the front of the stage. A set of microphones had been placed at a lower level so I could answer questions directly from my wheelchair.

I was tempted to turn back. How could anybody be ready for this? Cannon had explained that the conference was about to be broadcast live on every major television network in the world. With translations from English into every other major language. I was about to be presented as the first human born on Mars. Someone who could control robots by a hookup to his brain. Billions of people were about to see my every nervous twitch and hear my every nervous stutter. Both the mysterious nurse and the general had warned me that my life would never be the same after this.

Soon the world would know about robot control. The secret would be out. *Would it be worth the risk to me personally?* I wondered. Yet somehow I couldn't help but hope that letting the secret out to the world would buy my father's safety and allow him to come out of hiding. If what the nurse had said was true and he was alive.

"I'm ready," I said.

We reached the microphones as murmuring grew louder among the dozens of media people. Lights kept flashing from different cameras.

"Ladies and gentlemen," Cannon began in his deep voice, "I will begin with a prepared statement. Any questions following will be directed to me first. Those that I find suitable I will allow Tyce Sanders to answer."

"Why not let him decide for himself?" a raspy voice called. It came from a skinny man with a wispy gray beard who wore a tweed sport coat with blue jeans. "We heard rumors he's the reason the nuclear plant didn't blow. Like he's some kind of freak!"

The general smiled at the man. But it was a cold smile, and I was glad it wasn't directed at me. When he pointed at the man who had shouted out, a soldier walked up to the man, tapped him on the shoulder, and then escorted him out of the room.

"As you might guess," Cannon said as the door closed, "I intend for this to be a civilized event. Tyce hasn't spent much time on Earth. So we *will* be respectful of him and make his transition into public life as dignified as possible. Am I clear?"

Silence hung among the group of grown men and

women, as if the general were a strict teacher addressing a classroom of young children.

"Thank you," the general said after a weighty pause. "Let me begin."

Reaching inside his jacket, he pulled out a pair of glasses and placed them carefully on his face. Then he leaned forward and read from a sheet on the podium in front of him. "As you all know, two days ago a nuclear plant near Los Angeles, California, came within a half hour of catastrophic meltdown. Millions of lives were at stake. Millions more would have been affected for generations by the DNA mutations and cancer of radiation poisoning. The environmental disaster would have been one of this century's greatest tragedies. Yet the meltdown did not happen. I know there has been intense media curiosity on how the disaster was prevented. Today you will get the answer."

Murmuring began again, growing louder and louder.

Cannon waited, as if he knew there was no way to prevent the murmuring.

I'd read some of the headlines. Little had been revealed to the public yet. The Combat Force officials had decided to wait until they knew I was in good enough health to hold this conference.

Cannon resumed speaking into the microphone. "Essentially we were able to send a robot into a situation where no human would have survived. And at the same time, we were able to send a human in where no normal robot would have had the intelligence or flexibility to handle the situation. How did we do both at the same time?"

Another pause.

"This young man in front of you is able to control a robot with a hookup that links his brain and a computer. The computer in turn transmits his brain waves to the robot, so that it moves the way a body moves as commanded by the brain. The computer also sends information from the robot back to his brain. In short, it is virtual reality taken one step further."

Now the murmuring became open, excited conversation among the media members. I understood. It had only been a little over nine months since I'd learned about robot control myself, even though I'd practiced virtual-reality simulations as far back as I could remember.

"Our press secretary will give you handouts at the end of the conference," the general said. "These handouts detail many of the technical aspects involved in robot control. Let me say now, however, that it took old-fashioned human courage for this young man to prevent the nuclear plant meltdown. And to counter any critics of this new technology, let me be very quick to add that this is the philosophy of the World United Federation's approach to robot control. The robots themselves are no different than any other tool we use—from a hammer to an airplane. It is the human behind it who matters."

General Cannon stopped to take a drink of water from a glass under the podium. Then he removed his glasses, folded them neatly, and slipped them back into his pocket. "And now, let me introduce to you the first human born on Mars. Tyce Sanders."

With that, the eyes of the entire world turned upon me.

CHAPTER 6

I did what any normal human would do in front of billions of people.

I froze. Except for a smile that felt like someone was putting a finger in each side of my mouth and pulling. I didn't know if I was supposed to speak, so I just kept smiling at the reporters. I hoped I didn't have any particles hanging out of my nose.

"General, with all due respect to Tyce Sanders," one reporter said, "we can plainly see he is in a wheelchair. Was this a result of the nuclear plant accident? Did anything go wrong during his handling of the robot? Was he injured as a result?"

"No, it wasn't the result of the nuclear plant accident," Cannon stated. "No, nothing went wrong during his robot control. And no, he wasn't injured as a result."

That was true in one way. But in another way, I *was* in a wheelchair because of robot control. For when the pioneer operation had been done to my spine to allow the computer hookup to my nervous system, something had gone wrong. And because it took place on Mars, the doctor didn't have access to the specialized equipment he needed to fix the mistake immediately. That mistake left me in my wheelchair. I couldn't remember ever walking or running. It used to make me angry. But I was slowly learning how to live with it.

"Yet we heard he was hurt," another reporter said. Her white-blonde hair and red dress stood out from the pack. "We heard he's been in a hospital and—"

"Recovering from an exhausting rescue effort," Cannon said. "Tyce is in perfect health. Just tired."

"General," a taller man said, "I would guess until today this has been top secret. How much money has been spent on this robot-control research?" He chewed on his pencil while waiting for a response.

"It's in the report."

"Did the Federation approve this money, and if so, why wasn't it subject to public debate?" the man threw in quickly.

Cannon had warned me this type of question would arise. He took it without flinching. "Surely you understand that every government has issues of national security. This was one of them."

"Did Tyce Sanders have a choice in the operation?" the pencil chewer asked.

For a moment, Cannon paused. It was a moment too long. Because his brief silence said everything. I had not had a choice.

"The operation that allows the spinal hookup to a computer must be done before the child is three years old," Cannon said slowly. "Otherwise the neuron connections won't grow into place. We had the consent of his mother, who is involved in the Mars Project."

I coughed discreetly. Cannon looked at me.

"May I answer?" I whispered.

The general nodded.

Barely enough moisture remained in my mouth to swallow back my nervousness. What would I say in my first words to the world?

"Because of the operation," I said, "I'm able to see and hear worlds that no human has ever been able to explore. Outer space. The surface of Mars. I don't think there's a person alive who wouldn't want to have the chances I've been given as a result."

There was more to say, but I kept it to myself, because it was private. Dad had been off on a flight to Earth when my mom had to make the decision. Because the Mars Project hadn't counted on babies in its early stages, my mom was given a choice. Either she could send me back to Earth on a spaceship and risk what the g-forces would do to a baby, or she could allow me to have the operation and stay with her on Mars. So she made the best choice she could. No one guessed that something would go wrong during the surgery and that my legs would be paralyzed as a result. What's helped me deal with it is knowing that there's a God and that even when things look bad, he's still in control. He can make good things happen from bad things. Like the ability to travel the universe through controlling a robot with my brain. . . .

"General! General!" an African-American woman in black pants and a black sweater interrupted.

"Yes, Ms. Borris?"

Ms. Borris! Earlier Cannon had told me that Ms. Evangeline Borris was the most feared reporter in New York City. As a young reporter, she'd broken a story that overthrew a presidency. She was a legend now and not even that old, Cannon had said grimly. But Cannon had not described her to me. And when I saw her now, I gripped the arms of my wheelchair and tried to hold back my surprise.

It was her! Put on the platinum wig, smear lipstick across the lower part of her face, and it was the mysterious nurse who had visited me in the hospital! Only now she was the picture of dignity.

She spoke calmly. "If this young man can control a robot

capable of going places humans can't, wouldn't he make an ideal soldier?"

A hush fell on the reporters. They all looked at the general.

"He is not a soldier, Ms. Borris," Cannon answered.

"Are there others like him?" she asked.

"Ms. Borris," he said firmly, "for reasons of national security, I cannot—"

"Can you tell us about an incident on 04.01.2040 at the World United Federation Summit of Governors?" she persisted.

My guess was that only someone like Ms. Borris dared interrupt the general, for he didn't give her the same cold, hard stare he'd given the man who had been escorted out. Instead he seemed to squirm.

"And can you confirm or deny rumors that robot soldiers were involved in an assassination attempt?"

"Unlike you," Cannon said, biting back his anger, "I am not in the business of selling rumors to the public. Again, for reasons of national security, I cannot confirm or deny."

Muttering grew rapidly through the crowd, moving like a wave of water. Cannon had not denied it. And I guessed Ms. Borris was not known for asking questions unless she had a good source. To all the reporters, then, the general's refusal to answer said a lot.

"And lastly!" Ms. Borris now had to shout to be heard. When the others realized she wasn't finished, they quieted instantly. "General, is it true that children have been forced into robot control as slaves in a tantalum mine on the Moon?"

"Ms. Borris," the general said, the intensity of his voice like the crack of a whip, "I thought a respected reporter like you would not have to stoop to creating your own headlines to sell newspapers."

"Yes or no, General," she insisted. "Child slavery? If a child like Tyce Sanders is able to control a robot, who controls the child? And who controls those who control the child? Especially if the interests of national security make it so possible to keep this secret?"

The general drew a deep breath. "Interesting speculation, Ms. Borris. Perhaps you might be on the verge of a new career as a fiction author?"

"Hardly," she snapped back. "Not when this is far more bizarre than fiction. My sources tell me—" She didn't get a chance to finish.

Without warning, four soldiers stampeded through the middle of the crowd, shoving reporters in all directions. Without hesitation those soldiers leaped upon the stage. Two of them grabbed me out of my wheelchair. The other two yanked the wheelchair away and began running with it.

I watched helplessly as they sprinted toward the nearest exit with my wheelchair, leaving me behind. My feet dangled off the ground as the two soldiers held me by the arms.

"Hey," I said to the nearest soldier. "What's the—?"

"Not a word in front of the cameras," the soldier growled. He leaned forward and whispered in my ear. "There's a bomb. In your wheelchair."

The wheelchair they had run with.

Ten seconds later a loud boom from outside shook the entire room.

CHAPTER 7

"Tyce, what do you think we're up against?"

This came from Cannon. He and I were in a huge Combat Force helicopter, skimming along the Atlantic shoreline as we flew from New York City to Washington, D.C., where I was supposed to meet with Ashley before we moved to a Moon shuttle launch site in Florida. The roar of the engines was far too loud for us to talk without help of the headsets both of us wore. The vibrations of the helicopter engines rumbled through my body as I answered the general's question.

"We're up against someone wanting me dead," I said. Only a half hour had passed since soldiers had whisked all of us out of the media conference center. I was still shaky. I sat in a new wheelchair, taken from a hospital. It had no electric motor. And it seemed far too heavy with Earth gravity.

"What else?" Cannon said.

"There's your son," I answered. "He's still missing. I know you want to find him."

Cannon nodded. Beyond his large, square head, I saw the endless blue of the ocean through the window of the helicopter. All I had to do was turn the other way to see the green and brown of the shoreline, with the ribbons of highway and an occasional inland city.

"I want my son," the general said. There was a catch in his voice. "Nothing is truer than that. Just like the robot kids want to find their parents."

It hadn't been that long since Cannon had discovered his son was still alive. Although it appeared he'd drowned in a boating accident, Chad's body had never been found. Then one day a stranger had walked up to the general on the street and told him that Chad was alive and being held hostage. Once Cannon found out about the robot control, he assumed the robot-control operation had been done to his son too. Just like it had been done to hundreds of other kids across the world, all kidnapped in situations that made it look like deaths where the bodies couldn't be found. And each of those kids was a child of a high-ranking politician, World United Federation official, or Combat Force general.

Twenty-four kids made up each group, called a *pod,* and there were 10 pods total. Nine of the pods of kids had been rescued. But when they arrived at the location of the

10th pod, the jelly tubes were empty. Those were the kids who were probably on the Moon, held hostage to do tantalum mining.

"Yet," Cannon said, interrupting my thoughts, "this is even bigger than what matters to you or me. Or for that matter, to all the other robot-control kids."

The nine pods of rescued kids were now safe in the mountain retreat in Parker, Arizona. There the Combat Force was conducting DNA tests on their blood samples to help match them to their parents. Most of the kids were still in shock, for it was only recently they'd found out their parents were alive. They'd assumed they were orphans. Ashley too. She could have had the DNA test in D.C. but wanted the chance to be with some of her pod brothers and sisters before she went to the Moon with me to look for the last pod.

As I was thinking this, Cannon stopped speaking, as if he, too, were lost in thought.

I let my gaze drift to the horizon of endless ocean. It fascinated me. All that water, when on Mars there was nothing. No water. Which meant no life. Why was it that Earth had that one-in-a-hundred-billion-billion-billion chance that led to the right combination of sunlight and water and oxygen that allowed life? Most of my life involved science of one sort or another, so I thought about this a lot. Some people believe this happened through random chance. But for me, the more I learned about science, the more it pointed me toward God.

"Tyce."

I looked at Cannon.

"I wish I could tell you more of what's happening," he said.

"What's happening?"

He looked sad, tired. "There's some unfair stuff that I . . ." He took a breath. "Look, about the bomb. Don't worry. All right?"

"But it was a big bomb. Bad bomb. Like blow-up-and-make-lots-of-noise bomb. I—"

"Don't worry. That's all I can say."

This is what he'd been thinking about? That I shouldn't be afraid of bombs? Before I could say anything else, our pilot interrupted.

"Sir." Our pilot tapped his own headset. "There's an incoming call for you to take."

"Excuse me," Cannon said. Then he switched to a different channel and began speaking into his headset.

I thought of Ms. Borris. How did she know what she did? And that led me to thinking about her question about kids as slaves. Of anyone in the world, Ashley and I knew what that meant, for we'd seen it firsthand in the kids in the jelly tubes in Parker, Arizona. Even more than that, Ashley herself had been part of the Arizona pod before Dr. Jordan forced her to go with him to Mars for the deadly Hammerhead torpedo mission.

Suddenly the roar of the helicopter's engines seemed to

drop. *Strange,* I thought. *We're still above the water.* The D.C. base wasn't anywhere in sight.

Then my stomach rose to my throat. The helicopter had just pitched straight sideways!

Wind hit my face.

I looked away from the general and saw that the pilot's door was wide open. With the pilot gone!

Then the roar of the engines stopped completely.

With all the power off, the helicopter began to fall toward the ocean!

CHAPTER 8

There it was. Our helicopter. Tumbling. Tumbling. And at the last minute, just above the water, straightening. And leveling.

On television, it didn't look real. But seeing it—even from the safety of my wheelchair in a secure room on the D.C. Combat Force base—brought back to me the horror of thinking we were about to hit the water at well over 100 miles an hour.

"Wow," Ashley said from her chair beside me. "Heaven's going to be a great place. But let me be selfish here. I'm just glad you're not there yet."

It *was* good to be alive. And good to be with the only friend my age I had. Ashley was a year younger than me, nearly 14. With her short, straight black hair and almond-shaped eyes that squinted when she grinned, she looked like a tomboy. But when her face was serious, she could have been a model from the cover of a magazine.

Although Ashley and I had only met a little over nine months ago when she'd arrived on my dad's shuttle to Mars, we had become close friends quickly. We'd been through a lot together in that short amount of time. I could really trust her, and she trusted me.

"Wow is right," I agreed. Even though it was the next morning, I could still feel the sensation of falling toward death.

The television announcer's voice broke in as the clip of the tumbling helicopter ran twice more. "Although General Jeb McNamee, known as Cannon by his military comrades, had not been behind the controls of a helicopter for more than 20 years, he was able to avoid what would have been certain death for himself and Tyce Sanders. It is speculated that the pilot who abandoned the helicopter parachuted to a waiting boat. Neither the pilot nor the boat has been found, but author-ities are certain this assassination attempt is linked to the Terratakers, the worldwide terrorist group that reflects much of the world's opposition to outer space expansion. This was the second attempt in one day to assassinate Tyce Sanders."

There was a quick close-up of me looking into the cam-era, taken at the media conference yesterday, before the bomb blew. I was grateful not to see anything hanging from my nose. But I hated the goofy smile I wore.

"Reaction around the world shows mounting sympathy

for the World United Federation's Combat Force, a military organization that, until now, few people seemed to like. But when the Terratakers try to kill a teenager, it should be no surprise that they lose some of their popular support. Now to New York, where our network political analyst has this to say."

The screen immediately showed a serious man in a three-piece navy blue suit holding a clipboard. "Yes, Fred. As our viewers probably know by now, the first assassination attempt occurred less than an hour earlier yesterday at a news conference in New York City. There Combat Force officials had just announced to the world the incredible ability of Tyce Sanders to handle a robot by hooking up his brain to the robot's computer. As if this unveiling of technology that fuses human with machine wasn't enough to get the world's attention, it was also announced that Tyce Sanders had controlled the robot that prevented a nuclear plant meltdown outside Los Angeles earlier in the week."

The analyst's image faded as the network logo appeared on the screen. A deep voice said, "Robot control. Colonization of Mars. And terrorist assassination attempts. More on this when our one-hour special returns. . . ."

The television image switched quickly to two women in business suits. One sniffed under her armpit, hoping the other wouldn't notice. But the other woman did notice and began to recommend a brand of deodorant.

"Strange planet you live on," I mentioned to Ashley. "Life

or death situations on the news. With breaks to bring us really important things, like controlling body odor before important meetings."

"I've been meaning to talk to you about that serious issue," she said, grinning and plugging her nose. "Now what was the name of that deodorant you could use so badly?"

"Ha-ha."

We were interrupted by the opening of the door.

Cannon moved into the room. "I'm sorry I had to leave you two alone for so long. But I knew you would be safe here." Then he paused and sat down next to Ashley.

I knew something was up just from the way he sat down.

"Ashley," he said slowly and kindly, totally unlike his normally brusque self, "I have some news for you. The computers have been humming 24-7. They now have a match to the results of your DNA tests."

"My parents?" Her voice trembled.

He nodded.

Ashley's eyes widened, and she turned to look at me.

I was as startled as she was. After all, Ashley had spent her entire life thinking she was an orphan and had only recently been told by Dr. Jordan that her parents were alive. Now we knew it was true.

The look in her eyes was a mix of fear and excitement. *What will they be like?* it seemed to say.

My stomach fluttered nervously for her. What would it

be like to find out you had parents after all these years? And to finally meet them? Then another thought struck me. *Will it change Ashley's and my friendship? What if her parents don't want her to return to Mars? Or she decides to stay with them and not go?*

"Ashley? You okay?" the general asked.

Ashley just nodded.

"They're here right now, ready to meet you," the general continued. He stood up, walked toward the door, and opened it.

I could tell Ashley was holding her breath.

A man and a woman stepped into the room. They looked approximately my parents' ages. The man was of medium height, with thick, dark curly hair. He looked stiff in tan pants and a golf shirt. The woman was petite and Asian like Ashley. She wore a red hat that matched her dress. Her eyes looked misty, as if she'd been crying.

They ignored me and stared at Ashley. They smiled, but with hesitation, as if they weren't quite sure how to react.

"Ashley, please say hello to your parents," Cannon said.

CHAPTER 9

Late night 04.05.2040

Before, I thought I was lonely. Before, when I remembered Mars and my mom there and how she and my friend Rawling McTigre were millions and millions of miles away. Before, when I hoped and prayed my dad was okay wherever he was. But before, even at my loneliest, at least I had my best friend, Ashley, nearby.

And now she isn't.

Or at least she won't be when her parents take her away.

In the darkness, I stared at my computer screen and rubbed my face. I had been given a standard sleeping room somewhere in the depths of the military base. Two soldiers stood outside in the hallway to guard my room. It felt like I was in a prison cell again.

I kept seeing Ashley's stunned face and feeling the grip of her hand on mine. *What would it be like,* I asked myself again, *to meet parents you didn't remember?* When she'd left the room with them, she'd stared back at me with a sad and scared face. I couldn't get it out of my mind.

As a result, I hadn't been able to sleep, so I'd decided to add to my journals. These had begun when the dome on Mars started to run out of oxygen. Mom had said it might be good for people on Earth to see life on Mars from a kid's point of view. Even though the dome had survived the crisis, I had continued with my journal entries. Although I'd never admit it to Mom, now I liked typing my thoughts. It helped me sort them out.

And now, at least, focusing on what to put in the journal might take my mind off my loneliness.

I began to type on the keyboard, trying to put together all the things Cannon and I had talked about in some kind of order. The things I'd been thinking about a lot lately.

Someone tried to kill me today. Not because of any-thing I've done, but because of a worldwide political divide that began before I was born. Because of water and food and energy shortages from massive population overgrowth, it became apparent that a nuclear war might break out and cause human extinction. Out of all the proposed solutions, two became popular enough for debate. One side said humans should seek to expand beyond Earth. The other side, which became known as the Terratakers, called for "drastic reduction of growth." They didn't want to waste valuable resources on space exploration.

I stopped. I felt like I was writing an essay as homework. But I knew it should be in my journal. Sometimes I daydreamed that my journals would survive on DVD-gigarom for hundreds of years and that far, far into the future, a kid like me might stumble across them and begin to read.

Whenever I had that daydream, I realized how amazing reading and writing were. Without them, humans would not be able to pass on much information from one generation to the next. And reading what someone wrote was like hearing them speak in your mind, no matter how much time and distance had passed. So, in a way, I had the chance to talk to someone hundreds of years in the future. If they happened to find my journals. . . .

So as I keyboarded, I began to imagine I was telling this directly to a kid living in another solar system. He or she might think this was so ancient, hearing about the squabbles on the tiny planet of Earth, billions of miles away.

But if it was ancient history to him or her, it was also important. Because if the Terratakers succeeded in stopping space expansion, the chance to read it from another solar system would never happen.

Fortunately, as the issue was debated country by country, the voters rejected mandatory population control. It was too dangerous to allow government officials to play God by deciding who lived and who didn't. So the end result was to expand beyond Earth. This led to a whole new set of problems.

The goal of expansion was only possible if all the countries in the world joined together. But none wanted to lose independence. In the end, the former United Nations became the World United Federation. But it was not a one-world government with a common currency and one leader. The political structures in each country remained unchanged, and each country elected and sent one governor to the twice-yearly Summit of Governors. As part of this, every country in the world signed a 100-year treaty pledging resources and technology to expansion on the Moon and Mars.

There was still opposition, however. It was costing billions and billions to support the Mars Project—billions and billions that tapped into Earth's

resources and made life more difficult for the growing Earth population. Which also meant higher taxes.
Many within each country did not like making the
sacrifice in this generation for the next. Because
they had been unable to get their way in the political
process, they turned to terrorism. They became
part of the Terratakers.

Now, it appears I am included among their tar-
gets. Me and kids like me who control robots are
the next step in space exploration. To stop expansion then, they have to stop us and—

Someone knocked on the door and I stopped keyboarding.

"Yes?" I called. I wasn't too worried. If the Terratakers
had somehow made it into the depths of the Combat Force
base and overcome the soldiers who guarded me, I doubted
they would have knocked before entering my room. "Come in."

The door opened.

I hit Save on my computer and spun in my wheelchair.

It was Ashley.

"Hey," I said.

"Hey yourself," she replied. "I didn't know if I'd have a
chance to say good-bye in the morning."

"Not a big deal," I said. Even though it was.

"Yeah. Not a big deal," she repeated slowly. "I'll only be

gone for a day or so. Cannon says he still needs me to help you on the Moon. After that . . ."

Something about the way she hesitated made me afraid. "After that?"

"Well." She paused. "I mean, these are my parents. If I go to Mars to help assemble the carbon-dioxide generators, I might not see them for years and years. Cannon says it will be up to me whether to stay or go."

"I see," I said. And if she stayed, I would not see her for years and years.

"It's unfair," she returned. "Even if I wanted to go to Mars—and I think I do—how can I reject my parents? I'd feel guilty all my life. But they don't seem like my parents. I hardly know them."

"You've spent almost a day with them. How was it?"

She shrugged. "They seem like strangers. We get along, but it's hard to find things to talk about. I guess I shouldn't expect anything different, though."

I nodded. "At least you'll have the next few days."

"I'll miss you," she said softly.

"Yeah." I stared down at my lap. "I'll miss you too."

"Pardon? You mumbled something."

I coughed. "I'll miss you too."

"You'd better." She grinned. "But I have an idea. Remember the ant-bot?"

How could I not remember? It was a miniature robot.

I didn't know its official name, but Ashley and I had always called it the ant-bot.

"In all the confusion when we got arrested after the trip from Mars, no one ever asked for it back. I've had it hidden with me the whole time."

That would have been easy enough. It was smaller than an ant, and on the outside it vaguely looked like one too.

"You want me to have it now?" I asked.

"No. I'm going to keep it with me. Tomorrow night, about this time, maybe you can visit. I mean, not you. But through the ant-bot."

"You got it," I said. I knew what she meant. "Tomorrow night."

She ran to me and kissed my forehead. Then she ran out of the room before I could say anything else.

In one way I felt good about that kiss on my forehead. And in another way, horrible. What if she decided not to return to Mars?

I shut my computer down. I couldn't sleep. But I sure didn't feel like writing any more journal stuff.

CHAPTER 10

A loud ring and a monotone voice woke me. I blinked until I was awake enough to realize it was the phone beside my bed, reporting that I had an incoming call. I groaned and reached for it. The alarm clock showed it was 5:00. As in 5:00 a.m. Hours before regular people woke. Unless there was a good reason for this call, I was going to be very grumpy with the person on the other end.

"Hello?" I croaked.

"Tyce."

I knew this voice! Instantly I was wide awake. With no thoughts of being grumpy. "Dad! Where are you? Are you all right?"

"You are mistaken. This is not your father. But I have a message for you."

"But—"

"Listen. When you have your upcoming interview, don't be afraid to tell her the truth. About anything and everything. Trust no one else."

Then silence.

"And?" I said. "Anything else you want to tell me?"

"Yes. Robots don't get headaches."

More silence. The person on the other end had hung up.

Slowly I placed the telephone back. I stared at the alarm clock and watched the red numbers change, minute by minute. But I wasn't really focused on the numbers. Not with the thoughts going through my head.

The man had said he wasn't my father. But I knew my father's voice. It couldn't have been anyone else. Plus, only my father would have told me that robots don't get headaches. It was a private joke. Very private. Robots aren't supposed to get headaches, but their controllers sure get them. And I'd had plenty of them from the short circuits I'd gotten on several of our missions together. Had he said that so I would know it was him even though he had just denied it?

If that was true, what was going on? And what was this about an upcoming interview?

"Tyce," Cannon said to me a couple of hours later.

"Yes, sir?" I had just eaten breakfast. Not tasteless

nutrient-tube food, like we got on Mars, but real scrambled eggs, bacon, and toast with fresh strawberry jam. We were in a cafeteria—except the general called it a *canteen*—that overlooked the Combat Force base's runway. I sat with my wheelchair directly facing the windows. I'd gone my whole life seeing that butterscotch sky and blue sun on Mars. I couldn't get enough of Earth's blue sky and yellow sun.

"So that Ashley will have all day today with her parents," Cannon continued, "the Moon shuttle is set for tomorrow afternoon. That will give her most of tomorrow with her parents too. In the meanwhile, I'll give you a briefing."

I watched a jet land. The wing flaps were extended. Its nose was tilted up slightly. When the wheels hit the runway, a puff of smoke briefly blossomed behind it. It was an incredible sight. No one in the canteen seemed to be paying attention.

"Briefing?" I'd seen ads on television about undergarments, but this . . .

He smiled, and his stern face relaxed. "Sorry. I keep speaking military around you. A briefing means an information session. We'll continue from what you already know. Essentially we've already dropped robots into place on the Moon. One for you and one for Ashley. The robots are hidden just outside the warehouse in the Manchurian Sector. You and Ashley will go into robot control from a ship in orbit around the Moon."

He grinned and shook his head. "You know, talking like

this shows me how old I am. When I was your age, a Moon trip was incredibly expensive. Now it's like flying a commercial jet. We've got entire communities established under Moon domes. I mean, the last 20 years have been amazing in terms of space exploration."

I nodded. Someone had told me that there were people alive who'd been around before cell phones were invented. I could hardly believe that.

"My father," I said. I had decided to keep the early morning phone call to myself. "Any word on him?"

"Nothing. Yet. Everything possible is being done. He'll be found. I can assure you of that. In the meantime, we do have someone to make sure no Terratakers cause you any problems. On Earth or in orbit. He's your new escort." He pointed over my shoulder.

I strained and turned to see a familiar face. "Nate!"

He was wearing a grin that matched mine, and his blue eyes sparkled.

"Good to see you, buddy," he said, rushing forward with his large hand ready to shake mine. "Scared up any gators lately?"

I'd first met Nate in the swamps of Florida, where he had almost been killed by an alligator. He, along with the general, had helped Ashley and me escape the Terratakers. His platoon buddies in the EAGLES, the elite division of the Combat Force of the World United Federation, had nicknamed him "Wild Man." When we met him, he had looked the part, with a big, bushy black beard and equally bushy long hair. Since then he had shaved and cut his hair. He'd swapped his tattered wilderness clothing for something fashionable and now looked very respectable. The things that gave his background away, however, were the bulging muscles of his chest and shoulders and arms. Not even clothing could hide that.

"Good to see you too," I said. I meant it. Crazy things had been happening, and having Nate around was like having an anchor in a storm.

"So," Nate said to the general, "what's first on our agenda?"

"Nothing much." Cannon smiled. "Just a committee hearing later this afternoon."

Nate made a gagging sound. "Committee hearing! I thought you didn't want to put Tyce's life in danger."

"Danger?" The general frowned.

"Danger. Committee hearings will bore anyone to the point of death."

"It should hold his interest," the general answered, with a twitch of a smile. "He'll be answering questions for a delegation from the ethics committee of the World United Federation. This robot control is as new to them as it is to the rest of the world."

Ethics committee? Was this the interview Dad meant?

The general turned to me. "Yesterday's news conference set off a chain reaction across the world. Politicians at all levels are getting concerned phone calls about the treatment of children who are 'attached' to robots. The ethics committee needs to hear from you in order to make some first-stage decisions on how to respond."

My face must have reflected my thoughts.

"Don't be nervous," the general commented. "They're on your side. They just want basic information about what it's like to control robots."

"Sure," I said doubtfully.

"And then there's an interview with Ms. Borris. You might remember her from the news conference."

An interview with Ms. Borris. Could this be the "her" Dad had referred to during that strange phone call a few hours earlier? If so, boy, did I have questions for her.

"It seems she wants to allow you to let the world know that it's not a bad thing to control robots. The interview will take an hour and—"

A soldier in a standard Combat Force jumpsuit rushed toward us. His hair was shaved close to his skull. Stopping a respectful distance away, he waited for the general to return his salute.

"Yes?" Cannon snapped off a quick salute.

"Sir, it's about the young Ashley and her family."

"Yes?" Cannon lost his relaxed air.

"First of all, I've been instructed to tell you that the DNA results were faked."

"Faked! Who did it? How?"

"I wasn't given that information, sir. But I can tell you why. You see, our surveillance team has lost them."

"Lost them! Impossible!"

"Sir, I've been told it did occur. I've also been told to relay this message to you. Sir, they think she's been kidnapped."

CHAPTER 11

An hour later, Nate began to blindfold me.

"Ready to find Ashley?" he asked. He was the only other person with me.

"Ready," I said, trying to calm myself. Questions raced through my mind. Where had she been taken? How? By whom? The Terratakers? What did they intend to do with her? Or was she even still alive? I didn't want to consider that possibility.

"Headset next," Nate said.

"Right."

I was on a bed in a safe room somewhere deep in the Combat Force base. In a pinch, I could do this in my wheelchair, but the bed was more comfortable. Nate had already strapped me to the bed. With the blindfold came total darkness. Soon, when he finished pulling a headset down over my ears to block all sounds, the only sensory input to my brain would come from taste and touch and smell. But there wasn't much around to smell and taste, and since I couldn't move, my brain had already accustomed itself to the sensation of the straps that bound me in place.

All of this was important. I needed as few distractions as possible, for I was about to enter robot control. My head was propped on a large pillow so that the plug at the bottom of my neck did not press on the bed. This hookup had been spliced into my spine before I could walk so that the thousands of bio-plastic microfibers could grow and intertwine with my nerve endings as my own body grew. Each microfiber's core transmitted tiny impulses of electricity through my spinal plug into a receiver. Then that receiver transmitted signals to the robot's computer drive. It worked just like the remote control of a television set, with two differences. Television remotes used infrared and were limited in distance. Just like with cell phones, this receiver was capable of trading information with a satellite that in turn bounced and received signals to and from anywhere in the world. And all at the speed of light, 186,000 miles per second. Since the world was only 25,000 miles around, it meant almost instant communication.

"Let me run a checklist past you," I said, facing upward in total blindness. It was something Rawling had always done with me on Mars. He said it was very important, for the same reason that pilots run checklists before flying—safety. Nate didn't need the checklist; it was more a reminder for myself. More than that, it felt familiar. I needed that right now, when everything in my life seemed up for grabs.

"Fire away," Nate encouraged.

"No contact with any electrical sources. Ever." Any electrical current going into or through the robot would scramble the input so badly that the signals reaching my own nervous system could do serious damage to my brain.

"Check," Nate said.

"Second," I said, "disengage instantly at the first warning of any damage to the robot's computer drive." My brain circuits worked so closely with the computer circuits that any harm to the computer could spill over to harm my brain.

"Check."

"Final one," I said. "Robot battery at full power."

"Um . . ."

"I don't know either. But it's part of my checklist. Ashley's got the ant-bot. I can only assume since she intended for me to use it that she made sure it would be ready."

"This ant-bot," Nate began. "You're not making this up. Right?"

In the darkness beneath my blindfold, I laughed. "Not making it up. If a person can control a full-size robot, why not a miniature one?"

That was one of the many exciting possibilities for robot

control. No computer ever built could rival the human brain. Through robot control, the brain gave commands to machines. Big robots. Microscopic robots. I'd once controlled a space torpedo. There was no reason robot control couldn't be extended to aircraft or submarines. "Robot control," Nate said. "Ant-bot. All of this really messes with my mind. You know, when I was a kid, virtual reality was still a primitive type of game."

"Yeah," I said, grinning from my bed, "but that was ages ago . . . back when people listened to someone like Justin Timberlake. Now he might be in an old folks' home somewhere. So just remember. You *are* ancient."

"Ancient, maybe. But much bigger than you. And trained in the use of deadly force. Don't forget that."

"Also sworn to protect me, not threaten me," I answered.

"After I put on the headset, can I tape your mouth shut too?"

I was glad for the joking around. It took away some of my fear about Ashley. But I couldn't escape one question. What if her kidnappers had found the ant-bot and I couldn't communicate with her?

The answer to that would arrive in the next few minutes.

"I'm ready for the headset," I told Nate.

I felt him gently place the headset over my ears. Now I was completely trapped in darkness and silence. Which meant my brain would only respond to the signals from the robot.

I waited for the sensation of entering robot control. A feeling like I was falling off a cliff into a pitch-black void with no bottom.

It came.

Blind and in silence, I fell and fell and fell. . . .

CHAPTER 12

Somewhere, on the other end of the satellite, signals bounced back and forth between my brain and the ant-bot's computer. I expected to "wake up" and see through the eyes of the ant-bot.

You see, with robot control, the information is simply sent to my brain from the robot's eyes and robot's ears. In turn, my brain sends the robot information on how to move, the same way the brain directs my human body when I'm disconnected from robot control. I see and hear what the robot sees and hears. It moves the way my brain directs. Temporarily, it's like my brain is inside the robot computer. All I have to do is mentally shout "Stop!" and I disengage my brain from robot control.

Strapped to the bed, I waited for the falling sensation to end and for light signals from the ant-bot to reach my brain.

But the blackness remained.

It was as dark to my brain as if I were seeing through my own blindfolded eyes. In fact, for a moment I wondered if I had even managed to successfully link a signal between my brain and the ant-bot. Perhaps Ashley wouldn't even check the ant-bot until the time we'd talked about—late tonight.

So I tested it by flexing my arms. I half expected to feel the pressure of straps against my skin. Instead I heard a tiny click, as if the robot's tiny titanium arms and hands had hit something metallic.

Which meant the link had been established. My brain *was* receiving signals from the ant-bot. That meant I needed to explore the world around the ant-bot.

Groping in the darkness, I felt around with the robot's hands. I slid backward. That was my own action. But I also felt the entire body of the ant-bot bounce up and down gently. This was happening *to* the ant-bot, not because of it.

So I was inside something that was being carried by someone. Hopefully that someone was Ashley.

My brain gradually adjusted to the signals reaching it, just like my own eyes adjusted to light. And far away I saw the tiniest crack of light.

I tried to reach it and was surprised to find it closer than I expected. I bumped into something like a tube.

Finally I realized.

It wasn't a tube but a hinge. With light coming through

the tiniest of openings provided by the not-quite-perfect fit of the hinge.

I was inside Ashley's locket. The one her "parents" had given to her when they'd come to pick her up from the Combat Force base. The one they said they'd given her as a baby, kept all these years they thought she was dead, and now were finally able to give back to her.

I assumed she was wearing the locket around her neck. Rumblings vibrated through it and my ant-bot body.

Sound!

Loud sound!

Mentally I adjusted the sensitivity of the ant-bot's audio input.

The ant-bot works like a regular full-size robot, except on a smaller scale. The video lenses zoom from telescopic to microscopic. It can amplify hearing and pick up sounds at higher and lower levels than human hearing.

As I lowered the volume, the rumbling stopped, and the words began to make sense.

"Can you untie my hands so I can go to the bathroom?" This was Ashley's voice.

"Bathroom. Again?" said an annoyed voice.

I immediately guessed she'd been trying to get away from them often to open the locket and see if I was operating the ant-bot yet. This time I'd be there.

"I drank a lot of water. And like I keep telling you, it's

not like I can jump out the window. Airplane bathrooms don't have windows. And you don't see me wearing a parachute."

They were flying.

Not good news. Every hour meant she could be another 500 or 600 miles farther away. In any direction.

There was good news, however. Back on the Combat Force base, computer experts were attempting to locate the ant-bot by tracking its satellite signal to the computer receiver on base. They needed three different satellites to link up and triangulate in order to locate the ant-bot's latitude and longitude and altitude. Because this triangulation wasn't instant, I needed to stay connected to the ant-bot.

"Don't bother arguing with her," another deeper voice said. "What's the big deal?"

"I don't trust her," the first voice answered. "Someone in her position should be more afraid. It's like she knows something we don't."

"We're untouchable," the second voice said. "No one is going to find us. Relax. Untie her hands."

I felt more movement as Ashley rose from her seat. At least that was my guess. Stuck inside her locket, I didn't have much to go on.

A minute later light hit me, so bright that I nearly fell backward.

"Tyce?"

Ashley's gigantic face blocked much of the light. Her nose looked like a mountain to me.

"Ashley!" I shouted as loud as the ant-bot would permit. Once she'd visited me with the ant-bot. She'd crawled close to my ear and spoken in the middle of the night. This was before I knew the ant-bot existed, and I'd wondered if God was speaking out loud to me. Ashley had enjoyed scaring me with a voice from out of nowhere.

"Tyce?" She lifted the locket toward her ear.

"Ashley!" My voice sounded very tiny and tinny. I hoped she could hear me above the airplane noise. "Ashley!"

"Finally," she said. "I've tried a dozen times!"

She held the locket so close to her ear that I could have reached up and grabbed one of her hairs. Only to me, controlling the ant-bot, it would have been like grabbing a thick, thick rope.

"They weren't my parents," she said. "They were actors."

"I know," I answered. "And I found out the doctor who supplied the false DNA test has disappeared. This was a well-planned kidnapping."

"Well planned is right," she added. "And planned right inside the military by World United Federation Combat Force soldiers. I'm on one of their jets right now. The sun is coming through the right-hand windows."

World United Federation Combat Force soldiers. So there *were* even more traitors in the military than I'd thought. And that meant . . .

"Good-bye!" I shouted into Ashley's ear. There was no time to explain.

In my mind, I gave the *"Stop!"* command.

And just like that, I ended robot control.

Leaving Ashley all alone on an airplane headed away from safety at hundreds of miles per hour.

CHAPTER 13

Fifteen minutes later I faced Cannon and Nate. Outside. Near the runway of the Combat Force base. With jets taking off and their engines howling.

"What's going on?" Cannon said loudly. "I thought you said you could find Ashley with that miniature robot." His last words ended with a shout, as he tried to make himself heard above the jet engines.

I pointed at the jet. "She's in one like that!" I shouted back. "And I needed to talk to you about it where no one could overhear us with electronic bugging devices."

"What!" Wind whipped at my hair and the general's clothes. Nate, like a solid rock, seemed untouched.

"I said I want to make sure no one can hear us!"

"I can't hear you!"

"Exactly!"

"What!" he shouted.

Finally the jet left the runway. Seconds later the noise began to recede.

"I wanted to be at a place where no one could overhear us with electronic surveillance equipment. Ashley says she was kidnapped by Combat Force soldiers."

"You made contact!" This from the general.

Nate had no expression. He just stood motionless, listening to our conversation.

"She's in a military jet." I told them what had happened.

"And you immediately left her—" Cannon frowned as he hesitated and thought it through—"because if someone in the Combat Force had taken her, that means someone high up must have ordered the operation. And that higher-up is working for the Terratakers. So if the triangulation was successful, and we learned Ashley's location and sent in soldiers to rescue her, then word of that would have reached the traitor, and he would be in a position to have his soldiers search for the ant-bot and move Ashley again before our soldiers arrived."

"Exactly," I said.

The general's frown deepened. "That fits. The fake reports are easy to deliver if someone on the inside wanted it that way. And the only way our surveillance could have lost her is if they let it happen. That's the trouble with a military organization with hundreds of thousands of soldiers who come from hundreds of different countries across the world. The strength of the structure is diversity. But that also leads to its weakness. More difficult to control. There are 60 generals of my rank. Any one of them could have his own power base to run a secret military operation. So all it takes is one general to believe in the Terrataker cause for something like this to happen."

"What next?" I asked.

"You're going to have to find her without the triangulation," Cannon said. "Which means we need to hope and pray that she stays alive long enough to tell you."

"Why?" I asked.

"Why hope and pray?" Cannon gave me a strange look. He knew what I believed about God.

"Sorry. I meant why kidnap her. She's just one of the robot controllers. There are all the other pods full of control kids. But they took only her."

"I wish I could answer that," Cannon said. "But at least all the others are safe. Can you imagine if the Manchurians got the Terratakers to regain control of them too?"

"In the meantime," Nate put in, "we've got to keep Tyce safe. If we can't trust our own people, who's to say he won't be kidnapped next?"

"Impossible." But Cannon's tone told us he didn't really believe it to be impossible.

"Sir, a faked doctor report and dropped surveillance.

I think there's enough of a hidden organization within the Combat Force to make anything happen."

"You're right." Cannon sighed. "But it's absolutely crucial that Tyce faces the ethics committee this afternoon. And does the interview with Ms. Borris this evening. But now that Ashley's been kidnapped and we don't know what the Terratakers are up to, it's important for Tyce to handle the robot on the Moon today to help us find those kids as soon as possible. Any suggestions on how to do all of those things within a short time frame, Nate?"

"I have an idea," I said.

Both of them looked at me.

"How long would it take to get me into space?"

CHAPTER 14

This is what it would be like to walk on the Moon, I thought in awe, four hours later as my robot rolled forward on the Moon's dusty-looking surface.

The first thing I noticed was the sky. Mars, where I was born, has some atmosphere. The Moon has none. Because of it, the sky was jet-black. It seemed like a blanket I could reach up and pull around me, with tiny white holes burned through the blanket by starlight.

And it was very quiet. With no air to transmit sounds, my robot's audio didn't even pick up the slight squeaks that usually happened as the titanium arms moved back and forth. There was no soft squishing sound as the robot wheels sank into the soil.

But it wasn't really soil. And, at extremely low gravity, the robot didn't sink far.

The surface of the Moon isn't like loose dirt you might walk through in bare feet on Earth. It's like gray baby powder, a talcum of the softest dust you might ever run through your fingers.

However, a half inch below the surface it felt like cement. Without air molecules to separate the dust molecules, the weight of my robot on the narrow wheels—even with the lower gravity—was enough to compact the dust. It would be the same for you walking on the Moon. You would sink that half inch in the powder and leave behind perfect footprints that would forever remain preserved, with the sharp edges of your tread never blurred by wind or water.

What I loved the most about moving across the surface of the Moon were the patterns of dust from my spinning wheels. With no air and no wind to affect it, the kicked-up powder slowly, slowly fell in perfect semicircles away from my wheels.

I could have rolled forward for miles and miles, enjoying the peace around me.

But I had a job to do.

Ahead was the low, flat building that I had seen on the slide show in the Combat Force jet with General Cannon. Parked outside, just like the photos I'd seen, were platform buggies that moved supplies in and out of the building.

I had my instructions. Get the robot body beneath a platform buggy. Secure it in place on an axle. And wait until the platform buggy brought the robot body inside.

Which I did. Successfully. Ten minutes later, my robot was hidden beneath the platform buggy.

But that was only the beginning.

When I finished, I called *"Stop!"* and all the sights and sounds and sensations delivered to me by the robot's video and audio outputs faded away. An instant later I saw the darkness of the blindfold over my own eyes and heard the silence of the headset in my own ears.

Because in that instant, my mind had traveled 125,000 miles from the Moon to where I was currently. Hung in a small space station in orbit halfway between the Moon and New York City.

And while I wouldn't be leaving the space station for the next while, I'd be bouncing back and forth to a lot of different places with different robots.

CHAPTER 15

Ten minutes later—with just enough time on the small space station to say hello to Nate and go for a bathroom and water break—and another 125,000 miles below, I began to speak through a second robot body in New York City to the ethics committee of the World United Federation.

Seven vice governors sat behind a long, narrow table, each with a brass-engraved nameplate resting directly in front. Beside each nameplate was a comp-board.

All of the men looked as gray as the surface of the Moon. And just as old. They appeared so similar that it was hard for me to distinguish between them. They all wore gray suits and had gray hair and gray beards. And their expressions were gray—no smiles, no frowns. Just wrinkles that seemed carved into their gray skin.

They stared at my robot, so it felt like they were staring at me.

My robot faced the long, narrow table.

"How much longer do we have to wait for the robot to start talking?" one hoarse voice said. This came from a man who sat behind the nameplate marked *Vice Governor Patterson.*

"Frankly," another vice governor named Calvin answered in an equally worn-out voice, "I think this is all hogwash."

Hogwash? These men washed hogs? They were vice governors, which was the position just below supreme governor. From the world's 200 vice governors, the supreme governor was elected every four years. If the other 193 were like these stuffy-looking old men, the world was in big trouble.

"I agree," Vice Governor Armitage said. "It's nonsense. Probably some Hollywood stunt to promote a new movie. Trying to tell us the boy is in orbit and will hook up to this robot anytime now."

Oh, I realized, *hogwash is nonsense.* Earth expressions were weird.

"If he does start talking, I'm going to have a difficult time believing it's him," Armitage said. "It looks like a praying mantis."

I knew I should speak to let them know I'd arrived, but I was curious to know which way this meeting might go. Armitage's comment didn't surprise me or hurt my feelings.

The robot's upper body did look like a praying mantis. It was sticklike, with a short, thick, hollow pole that stuck upward from an axle at the bottom that connected two wheels. At the upper end of the pole were a head and a crosspiece, to which the arms were attached. Four video lenses served as eyes, and three tiny microphones, attached to the underside of the video lens, played the role of ears, taking in sound. A speaker on the underside of the video lens that faced forward produced sound and allowed me to make my voice heard.

The computer drive of the robot was well protected within the hollow titanium pole that served as the robot's upper body. A short antenna plug-in at the back of the pole took signals to and from my brain.

Another vice governor—Michaels, from what it said on his nameplate—moved out from behind the table and shuffled toward the robot. He peered directly into my video lens. I could see the veins in his yellowing eyeballs.

The old man tapped the robot's forward video lens.

"Ouch," I said.

Michaels jumped backward, nearly falling.

Instantly the murmuring at the table stopped. Michaels inched away until he reached the table, as if he were afraid I would attack him.

"Hello," I said through the robot's audio. "I am Tyce Sanders. I am controlling this robot. General Jeb McNamee said you might be interested in speaking with me."

"We want to speak with Tyce Sanders," Armitage said. "Not a robot."

"I wish I could," I answered. "But—"

"Yes," Armitage said with an impatient wave. "General McNamee explained this situation. Something about the speed of light and trying to have you in two places at the same time. Still, the ethics committee is not to be trifled with."

"Yes, sir," I said. "It is necessary that I also control a robot on the Moon. It is a quarter million miles from the Earth to the Moon. So if I were on Earth, the signals would have to travel to the Moon and back. That would mean too much of a time lag, because even at the speed of light that half million miles takes a little over a second. Ideally, I should be orbiting the Moon so the signal would be almost instant. As it was, we settled on a halfway point. From that place in orbit, I can control robots on Earth. And also, later, on the Moon."

I didn't add that being on a small space station was also the safest spot possible. Terratakers would not be able to reach me. The 125,000 miles of outer space served much better than any moat around any castle. At least that was the way Nate had put it.

"Anyway," I finished, "there is a slight lag between sending a signal and the robot reacting, but it is workable."

"Sending a signal." Calvin peered at me with some suspicion. "Am I to understand this robot responds to your brain commands?"

"It was in the report," Patterson snapped. "Must you always waste our time like this?"

"I want to hear it directly from the boy." Calvin didn't seem disturbed in the least by Patterson's outburst. He must have been used to it.

I explained. All of it. With plenty of stops for more questions and interruptions. An hour later all of them finally understood the concept. The delays were driving me crazy. All I could think about was Ashley and how I needed to get my committee meeting, interview, and Moon mission over and get back to finding her as soon as possible. This wasn't like juggling balls, something I'd taught myself to do on Mars. I mean, drop a ball and no big deal. But could I live with myself if I made a mistake with what I was juggling now?

"Please," Patterson said with a sigh, "may we get to the important ethical questions?"

"Certainly," Calvin said calmly. "We're not here to waste time."

"Ahem." Michaels faked a cough. "Explain to us how it was that you asked for this operation that allowed bioplastic fibers to grow into your nervous system. I understand you were just starting to walk at the time."

"Yes, sir," I said through the robot. "But I did not ask for the operation."

Michaels made a note on his comp-board.

"Who authorized the operation?" Patterson asked.

"I believe it was the World United Federation, sir. The operation was very expensive, but it did get full approval."

"Let me rephrase," Patterson said. "Who allowed you to be operated on?"

"My mother," I said.

"So you had no choice in the matter."

"No, sir. But if they had waited until I was old enough to make the choice, I would have been too old for the operation. It has to be done at a very young age to allow the nervous system and bioplastic fibers to grow together properly."

"In other words," Michaels said to Patterson, "we have over 200 children who all had the operation done without their consent. And if we want to take advantage of this new technology, we will have to continue operating on children who have no choice. The world may be a better place with this new technology, but they'll pay the price."

"Sir," I said.

All eyes turned to the robot.

I continued. "Since I have been this way all of my life— at least as far back as I can remember—I have never thought of it as paying a price. Being able to explore outer space and Mars through the body of a robot has been something so great I can hardly describe it—"

"Really," Michaels said, cutting me off. His eyes turned flinty. "Because of the operation, you've spent your whole life in a wheelchair. You might know what it is like to walk on Mars or on the Moon, but you don't know what it's like to walk on Earth. So let me ask you this. If I could guarantee an operation that would allow you to walk but take away your ability to control robots, would you have it done?"

"That is an unfair question," I said, stunned. "I was the only one out of all the kids who suffered spinal-cord damage because of the operation."

"In the future, mistakes will happen again. Would you trade your robot control to be fully human?"

"Are you suggesting that because I need a wheelchair, I am not fully human?" I insisted as hotly as I could through my robot voice.

Michaels blushed. "Let me rephrase that. Would you trade your robot control to be able to walk? Would you allow us to operate on another child, knowing that this child, too, might suffer the same nerve damage you did?"

I couldn't answer. That would be like playing God with someone else's life.

After long seconds, Michaels sat back in his chair. "As I thought. I don't think we need to ask any further questions."

CHAPTER 16

Half an hour later my robot rolled in the low gravity and zero atmosphere of the Moon. In orbit, where my body was hooked to computers, I wasn't tired yet. I'd just been in New York through one robot body, and now I was back on the Moon through another.

Here, in the Moon dust, my robot couldn't show emotion, of course, but my own excitement was nearly enough that it bounced forward.

The plan had succeeded!

During my time with the ethics committee in New York, someone here on the Moon had moved the platform buggy inside the low flat building above the mining operation.

That meant they had also moved my robot inside. When I had entered robot control, my robot was already past whatever security system was guarding this warehouse. Amid all the activity inside, no one had noticed as I'd lowered the robot onto the ground and out from beneath the buggy.

There were probably two dozen men working in space suits. I assumed they came in daily from the closest sector of the Moon dome—the Manchurian Sector. The men were working at various tasks, but most were moving pallets of boxes from one end of the building to the other.

Then one man noticed my robot. He gestured at it from beneath his helmet, then moved it into an elevator. A short ride took me down. When the doors opened, I was in a gigantic vault. And ahead, I saw about 20 robots like the one I operated. They held equipment that looked like giant torches and were cutting out blocks of material. It was obvious that their work had expanded this giant vault to the size it was. I couldn't imagine how many months they had already been doing this.

It only took a couple of seconds to move beside the nearest robot.

"Hello," I said. "We need to talk."

The robot kept pointing the giant welding torch into the rock face.

"Hello!" I shouted. "We need to talk!"

Still it ignored me.

Then I remembered.

We were on the Moon. No air. Which meant no sound waves.

They couldn't hear me. I couldn't hear them. Was this rescue attempt over before it could begin?

"Nate!"

Almost immediately he removed my blindfold and headset.

"Back from the Moon already?" he asked. He unstrapped my arms and legs.

I sat up and rubbed my wrists. "I'm back." The familiar walls of the small space station loomed above me. Or below me. Or beside me. It was hard to guess. In space, there's no up or down or sideways.

"What did you find out?" Nate asked.

"We couldn't talk." I grinned. "But we could scratch in the Moon dirt."

It had taken a while, but I'd finally learned from one robot what I needed.

The kids weren't staying on the Moon. They were on a space station somewhere. In orbit around the Moon. The rest I could guess. It was just like the pod of kids we discovered in Parker, Arizona, where Ashley was before she came to Mars. They were hooked up on permanent life support, unable to move out of their jelly tubes, living only through their robots.

"So," I said, after I explained that to Nate, "let's go rescue them."

"Sounds good to me. I'll call Cannon and tell him what we found out."

"Just one little thing," I said. "Down on Earth where I'm headed next. That dumb interview with Ms. Borris."

CHAPTER 17

That evening, through the video lens of my robot, I stared directly into a television camera. Behind the camera was the operator, a skinny man with a ponytail who had only been introduced to me as Ben.

The robot was in a television studio. The backdrop behind it was of New York City at night. In front of my robot was a coffee table with magazines. In a chair beside the robot was the legendary Ms. Borris. She wore black again, and I overheard her joking to the cameraman that it was her favorite color because it helped her look slim. Her natural hair was curly and cropped short. It looked far better than the platinum wig had when she pretended to be a nurse.

I thought of the mysterious phone call. How I believed it had been my father telling me I could trust Ms. Borris. And how, if it *had* been my father, he knew the interview would be taking place.

"Remember," Ms. Borris told me, interrupting my thoughts, "normally this is taped. But there has been such a demand for this exclusive interview that we are going live tonight to our worldwide audience."

"How is my hair?" I asked. With my robot arms, I pretended to smooth out imaginary hair on the robot's head.

Ms. Borris smiled. It took away much of her fierceness. "Nice touch," she said. "I wish the camera had been rolling when you did that. It would be a great opening shot to this news documentary."

Live to a worldwide audience. I reminded myself to be careful of what I did and said through the robot.

"Ready?" she asked.

"I have a bunch of questions for you." I lowered the robot's voice. "When are we going to be able to talk about—?"

"Camera's rolling," Ben said. "Live in five . . . four . . ."

"Ready," I said. Cannon had insisted that favorable and immediate television exposure was probably more important to the future of robot control than the recommendations of the ethics committee of the World United Federation. If people saw that robots were nothing to be afraid of and if they saw good use for robot control, their mass opinion would force vice governors all across the world to allow more tax money to be spent on robotics.

The only trouble was the questions in the back of my mind I couldn't escape. Would I trade my robot control to be able to walk again? Would I allow an operation on another child, knowing that this child, too, might suffer the same nerve damage I had? I sure hoped Ms. Borris wouldn't ask those questions.

"Three . . . ," Ben continued to count down.

Ms. Borris calmly sipped from a glass of water and set it down.

"Two . . . and—"

Ms. Borris spoke directly at the camera, reading from a teleprompter that scrolled words on a screen in front of her. "I'd like to introduce to you Tyce Sanders. Well, not Tyce himself, but a robot that he controls. Later in our show, we'll give you some of the technical details that make it possible for a human to control robots. You may, however, already know some of this. As I'm sure you're aware, very recently it was the robot Tyce controlled that prevented a nuclear meltdown just outside Los Angeles."

Ms. Borris turned to me. "First of all, let's talk about the situation you're in right now. It will give our viewers a sense of the potential of robot control. As I understand it, because of threats upon your life, you currently control this robot from a space station that's in orbit between the Moon and Earth."

"Yes," I said. I explained that in the afternoon I had answered questions via robot for the ethics committee. I didn't tell her, of course, about my brief time on the Moon and what I had learned there.

"Let's get back to the ethics committee later," she said. "I'm fascinated by the fact that you can almost be in two places at once. Are you telling me that if you had access to 20 robots all across the world, you could go from one to another to another?"

"Yes," I said. "I cannot switch instantly, but it is possible."

"So you could speak to me here in New York and five minutes later speak to someone else in London, England? And then five minutes later, Paris? And so on?"

"If a robot was waiting in each place." I thought of the ant-bot in Ashley's locket. And wanted this interview to be over so I could try to talk to Ashley again. "Not much different than using a phone."

"Is it tiring?"

"Physically, it is not." I explained how, during robot control, I was totally motionless. "Mentally, I can last as long as I would normally be able to stay awake and concentrate."

And so our conversation continued. I answered questions about growing up on Mars. I told her how it felt to go into robot control and how it felt to come out again. I told her about the capabilities of robots. That took well over a half hour of interview time.

After a short break, she continued with her questions. By then I was totally relaxed.

"You were able to go into a nuclear plant under extreme conditions," she began.

"Actually, my robot was. I directed its actions."

"Of course." She smiled. "Tell me, Tyce, if a robot is that unstoppable, wouldn't it make the perfect soldier?"

"It makes the perfect firefighter. It makes the perfect worker in extreme weather conditions. It makes the perfect explorer on the Moon and on Mars," I explained.

"But . . ." She leaned in. A fierceness filled her face. "If there were 200 of you orbiting in space and all 200 of you controlled armed robots down here on Earth, wouldn't you be perfect soldiers? Don't you see potential danger in that?"

"Who would build the 200 armed robots?" I asked. "Who would put them in place?"

My question seemed to catch her off guard. "I suppose," she answered, "it would be military people."

"Then," I said, "maybe you should ask them those questions."

For a moment, she frowned. Then she laughed. "Good point. Let's get to the operation itself. I understand it must be done before children are three years old. With adults, for example, the nervous system is too fully developed and won't properly intertwine with the bioplastic fibers that deliver information to the brain."

"That is correct," I answered. Now it was coming.

"So this operation is done to children before they are old enough to decide if they want it done or not."

"Yes." What was I going to say if she asked me if I would have allowed it to be done to me?

"So what if kids were taken from their parents at a young age and put into robot slavery?"

This wasn't the question I expected. I hesitated too long.

"What if," she continued, "I told you information has reached me that exactly this has *already* been done?"

"Then I would say that anyone who has that information and is holding it back to get better ratings on a show instead of helping those kids is using them just as badly as the people who put them into slavery," I fired back.

I expected her to get angry.

Instead, she smiled. "You are exactly right, Tyce Sanders. And that is why, right now, to a live worldwide audience, our network is going to break an exclusive story on how kids forced into slavery and armed with soldier robots almost assassinated all the officials at the recent Summit of Governors."

On a nearby television screen, I saw that the show cut from our interview and began to roll with the news story.

"How do you know all this?" I asked Ms. Borris through my robot. We were now off camera. Her exclusive story was giving out top secret military information.

"I'll tell you everything," she said. The bright, sharp

expression on her face had been replaced by one of deep weariness. "Later tonight. If I'm not arrested by then."

"But—"

"Ten o'clock tonight. Make sure you return to controlling this robot. I'll have it all arranged so we can talk."

"Tonight?" There was Ashley. And the Moon stuff. "But—"

"Tonight," she insisted. "Your father's life depends on it."

CHAPTER 18

I had to remind myself that my body was remaining in one place, the nice quiet calm of outer space. Because everything else seemed like a whirlwind. The Moon. Then the ethics committee in New York. The Moon again. Back to New York for Ms. Borris. It was as hectic as playing a computer game full-time.

And now?

The visuals from the ant-bot brought a weird mixture of light and dark to my brain. At first, I had trouble focusing. It took some zooming out with the ant-bot lenses until I began to comprehend that I was not in Ashley's locket. It seemed like the ant-bot was screened from the light by something.

Hair?

"Ashley? Ashley?"

Without warning, brightness overwhelmed the ant-bot. It seemed like it was at the bottom of a tunnel.

"Hang on, Tyce."

Ashley! Talking to me in a whisper.

"I'm going to tilt my head and hold my hand below my ear," she continued to whisper. "Then crawl out onto my palm."

So it *had* been hair from her head that had screened the ant-bot from the light. And she had hidden me in her ear?! Gross.

My entire world shifted, and I struggled to keep the ant-bot balanced.

"Ready," she said.

So I crawled out of her ear and onto her palm.

Ashley held her hand in front of her face. I peered upward through the video lenses of the ant-bot. To me, her face seemed as big as the presidents' faces carved into Mount Rushmore. I'd read about them once on an Earth history DVD-gigarom.

"I'm glad you're back," she said. "Why did you leave?"

I explained.

"That makes total sense. And it's probably the best thing you could have done. They took me to the one place no one would ever look for me. I think our only chance is if they don't know you guys know."

"I don't have much time," I told her quickly. Ten o'clock, New York time, was approaching. I had to make sure I was in the robot in the television studio to talk with Ms. Borris. "It would be nice if you started making sense."

"Tyce," she said, sounding tired, "I'm back with all the other robot-control kids. In the mountains of Arizona."

"So you're safe, then."

"No."

"No?"

"I remember a story once," Ashley whispered, as if she was afraid of being overheard. "It was about a woman who was so scared of being robbed that she put bars on all her windows and a dozen locks on her door. Her house caught on fire, and she couldn't get out."

"Meaning?" I asked. I was conscious of how little time I had. "Help me out with your riddle."

"Meaning," she answered softly, "the perfect place of protection can also be the perfect trap. The Combat Force soldiers are in control of a fortress no one can get into. But no one can get out of it either. The only link is by telephone or computer. Combat Force soldiers at other bases have no way of knowing anything is wrong here if someone on this end of the communications system lies to them."

I had a horrible feeling. My earlier conversation with Cannon came back to me. The one where I'd asked why Ashley had been kidnapped if there were all the others.

And Cannon's words echoed through my mind: *"But*

at least all the others are safe. Can you imagine if the Man-churians got the Terratakers to regain control of them too?"

"What you're saying—" I gulped—"is that the wrong Combat Force people control this. And you're all prisoners."

She nodded. "The Terratakers have us again. They'll blow this place to shreds if anyone tries to take it. With us in it."

CHAPTER 19

When I left the ant-bot and began controlling the robot in
New York City at 10:00, Ms. Borris was not waiting for me
as promised.

Instead, when light waves reached my brain through the
video lenses of the robot that had been left behind in the television studio, I found the robot alone in a small room. In front
of a television.

I tried the door.

It was locked by a keyed bolt. No one could enter without the key. No one could leave without the key. The door was
a steel fire door. I doubted even a robot could break through.
What kind of trick did she think she was playing? I wondered.
Trapping the robot wasn't like trapping me. All I had to do
was disengage anytime I wanted.

Did she expect me to wait?

Or, it hit me, had she been taken somewhere so she couldn't be back on time? Had she been arrested, like she feared?

I looked again at the television and the remote sitting on top.

I wheeled over, took the remote, then backed away from the television. When I pressed the remote, the screen flickered immediately to life. Ms. Borris stared straight at my robot from the screen. There was no backdrop behind her. Just a close-up of her face, looking fatigued.

"Tyce," her television figure said, "earlier today I locked your robot into this closet for fear that right after our interview, I would be arrested by the Combat Force for the subjects we discussed on television. *Kidnapped* is a better word, because I have done nothing to deserve being arrested. I knew the questions I was asking you would get me into trouble. I prerecorded this in case that happened. If I am not speaking to you in person, then you know I am in trouble. The only way to safety for all of us is for you to bring the whole truth about robot control to the world by media limelight. Not even the Terrataker traitors within the World United Federation can fight massive public opinion. Thank goodness, democracy still rules."

Ms. Borris paused to lift a glass of water into sight. She sipped from the glass, then set it down out of sight again. "Let me start by telling you that your father is not who he appears to be. For years, as a space pilot, he has been working under-cover for the United States division of the Combat Force. As have I. We are both dedicated to stopping the Terratakers, and all of those aligned with the Manchurians who back them, from reaching world dominance within the Federation."

Dad? *My* dad? If robots could breathe, I'm sure mine would have held its breath as I kept watching through its eyes.

"General McNamee arranged for your father to escape the Combat Force prison in the Florida Everglades while you were in Arizona. In so doing, McNamee risked his career. There are higher-ranking generals within the World United Federation who do serve the Terratakers. If they found out he was responsible . . ." She took a deep breath. "You do know they are holding his son hostage."

Where was she going with this? And how did she know?

"The general is playing a complicated game," Ms. Borris continued. "The higher-ups put him in charge of the robot-control technology because they have his son as a hostage and know they can control him. They tied the general's hands by telling him next to nothing about the operation. This way it would look like officially they have done their best. Unofficially, they could try to stop him. Yet because of you and Ashley, he was able to prevent the assassination attempt at the Summit of Governors. They do not intend to let him go any further. He can't openly fight the Terratakers hidden within the ranks above him or they might kill his son. Nor can he openly divulge military secrets to the media as a result of the Combat Force oath he took."

Where had she gotten all of this information?

"That is why he arranged for your father's escape. Your father has been feeding me the information it will take to defeat the Terratakers through media publicity. Cannon can't speak directly, so he has funneled information to your father."

She knew where Dad was!

"You may also be aware of the highly sophisticated electronic listening devices available to the Combat Force. It wouldn't surprise me if one was attached directly to your clothing. Or your wheelchair. Anywhere that will let some of the Terratakers listen to any of your conversations. For that reason, the general has been able to say little to you. And for that reason, your father has not been able to contact you directly, except for that one phone call."

She took another sip of water. "He was hoping you would be able to visit him in a robot body, which wouldn't be bugged. But he was also afraid that something might happen to me or that somehow we might get caught together, so he has only contacted me via telephone or computer. I don't know where he is. I can only tell you what he told me. And that he is safe."

Ms. Borris closed her eyes briefly. She looked sad and tired. I think I understood why. She expected to be arrested any minute. That made it all the more brave that she had decided to videotape this message instead of fleeing to somewhere safe.

"You'll find your father at the place where he and Rawling hung out in New York during their training days."

Rawling? They knew each other before the Mars Project? What kind of training had they done together? My mind spun with possibilities.

"Your father says that Rawling won't give out that information unless he knows it's you asking. So even if the wrong people listen to this message, they won't be able to find him. But you can. Let me repeat. At the place where he and Rawling hung out in New York." Ms. Borris sighed. "With me gone, you're the link, Tyce. You need to get this story broadcast to the world. Then your dad can come out of hiding. And I will be released. If I'm still alive."

There was noise behind her. She whirled in the direction of the noise. Then back at the camera. She began to talk very quickly. "I trust Ben, my cameraman. He's promised to lock your robot in a closet with this video ready to play. I hear the soldiers coming now. Get the information from Rawling. Find your father. He's got a way to reach the world media. Understand? Get to your father."

But the door was locked.

She smiled on camera, as if reading my mind. "You'll find a key taped beneath the television. It will let you out of the closet. From there, get out of the building through a fire exit as fast as you can. And please, find your father!"

The TV went dark.

CHAPTER 20

"Nate?" It was my voice speaking, not a robot's voice. I wasn't seeing through a robot's video lenses in New York or in Arizona or on the Moon. I was seeing through my eyes, the ones that had been blindfolded to make my robot control easier.

"Nate?" Here on the small space station in orbit, my strapped-down body was helpless. "Nate?"

The part I didn't like about coming out of robot control was the waiting and wondering in the darkness and silence. I was totally dependent on Nate, the only other person aboard the small space station.

"Nate?"

What if he didn't answer? What if something had happened to him? What if he'd somehow died? I'd be strapped in place with no way to move my hands. No way to remove the headset or blindfold. I'd be trapped until I, too, died.

"Nate?" My heartbeat thudded in my ears. But that was the only sound I heard. "Nate?"

Seconds later he pulled my headset off. Then my blindfold.

"Sorry," he said as he began to unstrap me. "I was at the station's telescope. Took me a while to get here. I'm not that good at moving through weightlessness yet. You okay?"

"Could you leave the straps in place?" I asked. "I need to control a robot on Earth almost immediately."

"You have my full sympathy, bouncing around everywhere."

"I just came back because I need to use the computer," I said. "Can you move to the computer and let me dictate to you an e-mail from your address? With no questions asked? I don't have time to explain."

"Sure." His big smile was reassuring. He pushed himself away from the bed and toward the computer. When he reached it, he called over his shoulder, "Dictate away."

The computer had a permanent Internet connection via satellite. Without hesitation I called out my message. Nate began typing. When he was finished, he printed out a copy and brought it to me.

I scanned it to make sure it said everything I wanted. Dictating was more difficult than seeing the words on a screen.

From: "Nathan Guthrie" <guthrien@worldwidenet.com>
To: "Rawling McTigre" <mctigrer@marsdome.ss>
Sent: 04.07.2040, 09:28 P.M.
Subject: Where?

Rawling!
Ignore the sender address at the top. It's me. Tyce.
Remember, hard head against axle? No time to explain
much. I know about you and Dad. Please establish your
identity on a return e-mail by telling me where you hung out
with him in the downtime during your training sessions in
New York. Much to tell later.
Your friend,
Tyce

It was close enough. The "hard head" phrase would be
enough for Rawling to know it actually was me. Once, on a
mission on Mars, I had bumped the robot's head against the
underside of a platform buggy and made a dumb joke about it.

I didn't really need for Rawling to establish his identity
on his return e-mail. But I desperately needed to know where
they had hung out. By making it seem like I was merely doing
an identity check, it might throw off anyone who might inter-
cept the message. I couldn't risk someone else finding out that
was my next destination in the robot body I'd left behind with
Ms. Borris.

"Looks good," I told Nate. "Can you fire it to Mars?"

He nodded and returned to the computer. "Sent," he announced after hitting the keypad. "As promised, with no questions asked."

"Thanks," I answered softly. Mars was so far away that even at the speed of light, it would take a while for the message to cross the solar system and arrive at Rawling's computer at the Mars Dome. With luck, he'd be at his computer and could reply immediately.

In the meantime, however, I couldn't rest.

Nate had set up a meeting with me and Cannon.

Back on Earth.

CHAPTER 21

"No, Tyce," Cannon said to my robot, "we can't simply take over a space station."

I was controlling a robot at the military base in D.C., and we sat in Cannon's small office.

"Dozens of countries each have their own in orbit," he continued. "According to international law, a space station is an extension of that country's territory. Attacking a space station, then, is an act of war. That's why you're so safe in the small one with Nate."

"But that remaining pod is orbiting somewhere around the Moon, and it's got to be the one that belongs to the Manchurians. I talked to the kids through their robots. You're right. They're being held as slaves and forced to use their robots to work in the tantalum mine."

Cannon closed his eyes briefly. He rubbed his face. "My son is probably on that space station. Don't you think I want to begin a military operation to rescue him?"

"Then do it. Please."

"First," he said, "it would start an international incident that may lead to a third world war. At the very least it would destroy the Federation of countries that to date have somehow managed to work together in world peace and toward the colonization of Mars."

He sighed. "Second, even if I wanted to, there are still higher-ups in the military who would stop me. And third, even if I had permission, it would be an unsuccessful raid. The Manchurian space station's crew would have plenty of notice of our approach. All they would have to do is dump the kids into space. They would die instantly, float away, and we would never recover their bodies. We'd end up boarding an empty space station, and it would be a political disaster."

"But if you knew we could do nothing, why send me in a robot to confirm the robot-control slavery?" I wondered if my robot's voice reflected the stress I felt in my own body. It had been a long day, and it was now well past midnight.

"I was hoping," he said, "that the kids were somewhere on the Moon. Then it would have been far easier for a combat unit to approach quickly and unseen. And far more difficult for the Manchurians to move the kids or even hide their bodies."

"What you're telling me," I said through my robot, "is even though we know where they are . . . even though there's a real possibility that Dr. Jordan and Luke Daab are there too . . . still, we can't rescue the kids or capture Jordan or Daab?"

The general slowly nodded. "That's what I'm telling you. Unless you can think of something I can't." He stood. "And in the meantime, we have to do something about the other 216 kids now held hostage in Arizona. By our own Combat Force."

On my end, I took a deep breath. "Well, sir, I do have an idea about that. Would you be able to get some men loyal to you ready and waiting just outside the compound there?"

"Sure. We can have them there in an hour. Then what?"

"Hope and pray. In the meantime, I have a lot of robot control ahead of me."

I was about to disengage when someone knocked on the door.

"Sir?" The voice came from a man in uniform. I switched to a rear video lens and glanced at him. "Sir, I—"

"Not now!" Cannon barked at him.

It was too late for Cannon. The man in uniform had not guessed that I was currently controlling the robot. So I got a full look at the man's face.

It was the pilot! The man who had jumped out of the helicopter to leave us to crash! He was here? Working with Cannon?

"Tyce," Cannon said to my robot, "I can explain. Really."

I pretended I had already disengaged. If Cannon had double-crossed me, I didn't want him to know that I knew.

I woke up back on the space station. It was about 1:00 in the morning. And I was sick with worry.

Was Cannon on the Terrataker side? Would he have the Combat Force ready to help in Arizona? Or would he betray me?

"Nate," I called out, "anything back from Rawling on Mars?"

"Yup." Nate read me the e-mail.

"Next destination then, Nate." I grinned upward from under my blindfold. I had to pretend everything was fine. I also desperately wanted to sleep. But there was no time. "Keep me moving. Back to the robot in New York."

My robot rolled off the street into a crowded coffee shop. It seemed that many of the people sitting at the tables wore shabby brown clothes and held their cups of coffee in both hands as if afraid someone might try to take them away. Cigarette smoke hung in the air like swirling fog.

Upon my appearance the low murmurs of conversation instantly turned into silence.

I knew they were all gawking at my robot. Unless they'd watched a lot of television over the last few days, they wouldn't know about robot control. Even so, the reaction wasn't so unusual. After all, what would you think if a nearly six-foot robot rolled into a place where you were having coffee?

"Greetings!" I said. "Is this a good place to get a cup of warm engine oil?"

People stood nervously and edged away from me. Some fled the coffee shop.

One man in a ragged brown suit shuffled toward me. His shoes were almost worn out, and his face was hidden by a threadbare baseball cap. He got very close and whispered to my audio input speaker, "Engine oil? Couldn't you think of anything better than that?"

"Dad!" I whispered back. "It's good to see you!"

We sat in the backseat of a taxi. Dad pulled his hat away from his face.

My robot body was bent at the waist to fit in, with my wheels above my midsection. It was like I'd been folded in half.

The taxi driver had just grunted when we got in the car. Evidently seeing a weird-looking robot and a homeless man together didn't even startle him.

Dad grinned. "Taxi drivers in New York have seen every-thing at least twice." Then he turned serious. "I doubt we have much time. I'm sure your robot has been reported by someone who saw it roll from the television studio to the coffee shop. From there the authorities will start pursuit."

I'd already explained to Dad how I got the name of the coffee shop from Rawling by return e-mail. Dad had promised to tell me everything else. Later. But first he had hustled us into a cab.

"Where are we going?" I asked.

"A computer expert," he said. "Ms. Borris and I spent a lot of time thinking this through. I think we can do it. But you're going to have to learn fast."

"You're right," I said. "In about half an hour, I'm expected in Arizona."

I caught Dad's strange look out of the robot's side video lens.

"Long story," I said. "But I have to ask. Can we trust Cannon?"

"With our lives, Son."

If that was true, what about the pilot? But if there was anyone I would believe, it was Dad.

"Why do you ask?"

I answered, "I'll tell you more later. This is so complicated I hardly know where I am anymore. But if Ashley was able to get the ant-bot onto a soldier's sleeve like I asked just before getting into this robot, we might have a chance."

CHAPTER 22

"Mister," I said 40 minutes later, speaking softly through the ant-bot, "you have a lot of earwax."

I didn't know how Ashley had managed to get close enough to the soldier to put the ant-bot on his sleeve. All I knew was that she had done it. It had taken me 10 minutes to crawl up his sleeve. During that time, I'd heard three or four other soldiers address him as "Sergeant." So he was the one in control here. Ashley had picked the right person.

"Huh?" he said. "Who is that?"

"Does it matter? I'm inside your head." The sergeant did have a lot of earwax. I was very glad my ant-bot couldn't taste or smell. I had burrowed deep into his ear, deeper than any finger or Q-tip could reach. And I intended to stay.

"Who is it?" he repeated, with panic in his voice.

For the first time, even though I didn't quite know where this conversation was headed, I thought this crazy plan might work.

"Here's the truth," I spoke into the darkness of the bottom of his ear. "I am someone who can make your life miserable. Unless you listen to me."

"No!" The sergeant's panic grew. "It can't be you!"

I wondered who he thought I was. But I was willing to play along. "Why can't it be me?" I asked.

He moaned. "I swear I had no choice. I thought enemy soldiers were about to take us. I thought you'd run away with me. When I found out you hadn't, it was too late to return to help."

"Chicken," I said.

"Please," he pleaded. "I've already been tortured by memories of you begging me to come back. I didn't mean to leave you in battle. You don't need to haunt me more."

This guy believed in ghosts? "Just unlock the rooms that hold the kids," I said. "Let them outside in the open area. Then I promise to leave you alone."

"No!"

"Oooooooh!" I raised the ant-bot's voice and tried the corny spooky ghost voice that you sometimes hear in really cheesy horror movies. *"Oooooooh! Leaving me aloooooooone. Oooooooooooh!"*

"Please! Please leave me!"

I notched up the volume. *"Oooooooooh! Oooooooooooh!"*

"Ouch!" he cried.

"I think," I said, "I'll sing you some of my favorite songs. I know about 100 of them."

I felt his head move. The darkness of the ear got even darker, as if he had clutched his head with both hands.

"Old MacDonald had a farm," I began in my best off-key voice, remembering when Mom used to tell me about Earth tunes and other things on Mars. I still hadn't seen a farm or a pig or a duck, but I sure knew how to sing about them. *"Ey-iy-ey-iy-oooooh!* And on this farm he had a pig. *Ey-iy-ey-iy-oooooh!"*

It was fun, singing, and I hit it with gusto. "With an *oink-oink* here. And an *oink-oink* there . . ."

"No! Normie, don't do this to me! I'm sorry I let you die!"

"Ducks next," I promised. It was really sad that he'd abandoned a friend. Sadder that he had all this guilt. But the lives of more than 200 kids were at stake. I was going to push hard. "Do you like ducks? *Quack? Quack?* I'm going to be spending a lot of time in your head. Day and night. Unless, of course, you let the kids outside."

"I can't! I can't!"

"Mooo! Mooo!"

"Please don't do this to me," he continued to moan.

So I decided to try a different strategy. I reached out with one tiny ant-bot arm. Although I couldn't see what I was doing, I pinched as hard as I could.

"Ouch!"

I pinched and pinched. And *quacked* and *quacked*. And pinched and *mooed*. And pinched and *oinked*.

"Stop!"

I stopped.

"Just five minutes," he said. "If I let them out for five minutes, will you leave me alone?"

CHAPTER 23

"Here's the problem," I said to Nate back at the small space station when I had disengaged from the ant-bot. By now it was almost 2:00 on the morning of 04.07.2040. "Sound doesn't travel on the Moon. So I can't interview the robots in the tantalum mine."

It was a relief to be away from robot control, at least for a while. I was glad to be floating in the zero gravity of the space station. On Earth, 125,000 miles below, if one plan had gone right, Ashley and all the other kids were now outside the Parker, Arizona, mountain fortress and about to be rescued by Cannon's commando unit. If another plan went right, Dad and the computer expert guy in New York had used an access code given to Dad by Ms. Borris to get into a worldwide satellite feed that would also connect to the computer on Nate's and my space station. On this end, all I had to do was enter the access code they had given me.

"Interview?" Nate had not shaved since we'd left Earth by shuttle. He rubbed the beginning of the dark bristles on his chin as he gave me a quizzical look.

"Cannon said there was no way to send in a military force." I grinned. "So let's send in the entire world." I looked down at the space station's mainframe. It didn't take long to keyboard the right access code. But I was far from finished.

"Send in the entire world?"

The next part was tricky. It involved tinkering with connector cables and hardware. I knew I needed to concentrate, but I was so tired that it felt like I was wearing heavy rubber gloves. That's where robots have a distinct advantage. They never get tired. They go until they run out of battery power, then stop. Me, I needed sleep.

I rubbed my eyes and strained to look for the right plugins. I needed to connect the mainframe to the robot-control computer. No one had ever tried this before, but the computer expert thought it wouldn't be a problem. Of course, he wasn't on a space station halfway between Earth and the Moon. Nor was he the person about to hook himself up to both computers.

"Ey-iy-ey-iy-oooooh . . . ," I hummed to myself. Anything to stay awake. Somehow the tune had stuck in my brain, and I was having a hard time getting it out. "With a *moo-moo* here. And a *moo-moo* there. *Ey-iy-ey-iy-oooooh . . ."*

"Tyce!" Nate's voice broke in.

"Huh?"

"You all right?"

"Yeah." I snapped a connection in place. If I had it wired right . . .

"You didn't answer my question. Send in the entire world?"

I rubbed my face again. "Virtual reality. It's like the real thing."

"Pardon?" Nate asked. "You're slurring your words."

I slapped my face a few times. "Virtual reality. We send the world there. Or we send there to the world."

"Buddy, I'm worried about you."

"I'm worried about me too," I said. All I wanted to do was sleep. But I couldn't. Five minutes. That's all I needed. Five more minutes of staying awake. "Can you help get me ready for robot control one last time?"

Back in the tantalum mine, I found the robot exactly where I had left it. In the shadows of a man-size hole gouged into a shaft dug by other robots.

I rolled forward.

All of the other robots were busy with their giant torches. Except for a video monitor, they were not under supervision by any adults in space suits.

This made sense. The kids themselves were held

hostage on the Manchurian space station. They had no place to escape, no matter what the robots they controlled on the Moon below them might do. So why waste space-suit time for adults? Just give the kids their assignment and work them mercilessly. The whole thing made me feel sick.

When I reached another robot, I touched its arm with mine.

The robot stopped cutting into rock.

It watched as I bent over and scratched some words on the Moon dirt, glad that English had evolved into a standard language across the world. These kids had all been kidnapped from different countries and had been robbed of the one place most important for anyone. Home. Something that maybe they'd finally find if we could get them released.

I finished scratching and let the kid who controlled the robot see what I had written. The robot clapped. The movement drew other robots closer.

Finally all of them crowded around to read the ground. And all started clapping. It had only taken four simple words.

Time to go home.

CHAPTER 24

Suits. I had never worn one on Mars. So this was a first. I decided I hated them. Especially stiff navy blue, with a white shirt underneath that itched. And a tie that cut off my air supply. I was glad it wasn't standard issue on Mars. But Ms. Borris had knotted the tie for me and told me to quit fussing. Dad had laughed the whole time I had tried pushing her away.

"Showtime," Ms. Borris said, with an uncharacteristic grin on her face.

"Wonderful," I said. I made a face at Ashley. She knew what I meant. It was anything but.

Yesterday, two hours after my robot had made contact with the other robots at the tantalum mine, a space shuttle had taken Nate and me back to Earth. After a quick flight to New York, I was ready—finally—for a good night's sleep.

This morning, the most wonderful thing happened. I woke up to my dad's smiling face.

And now I was about to face the World United Federation ethics committee—again. But at least I knew what to expect from the vice governors this time.

The door to the waiting room opened, and a Combat Force soldier nodded in my direction.

Dad knew better than to push my wheelchair for me. I hated it when anyone did that. It made me feel weak and helpless.

I gripped the arms and rolled forward. Alone. And nervous, yet somehow confident too.

The decision of the ethics committee would determine the future of robot control. Which would determine the direction of human history. I guess that was important enough to wear a suit. Even if it was uncomfortable and itchy.

I passed through the door and moved down the hallway.

The Combat Force soldier escorted me into a quiet chamber where all seven gray-haired men waited for me. The chamber where I had already faced them as I controlled a robot.

Now it was me.

In my wheelchair.

In my suit.

Showtime. None of the vice governors spoke for the first five minutes.

Instead the lights were dimmed and footage played on a large screen at the front of the chamber. I knew the footage. It had played for the entire world the day before, while I was still in the space station halfway between the Earth and the Moon.

It showed the interior of the Manchurian Sector space station that orbited the Moon. The kids were lined up in neat rows, suspended in giant jelly tubes.

A voice-over played during this eerie scene. "My name is Ingrid Sosktychek. I am 12 years old. When I was too young to remember, I was taken from my parents. I was trained in robot control on Earth. Two years ago I was moved here onto this space station. Twelve hours a day I control a robot that digs rock in a mine on the Moon. For the other 12 hours I am put to sleep and fed through tubes. Twice now my body has outgrown the tube that holds me. There are 24 of us on this space station. Please help."

The footage showed as much as Ingrid could see through her own eyes as she turned her head within the tube that held her body. Then it went blank.

The blankness didn't surprise me. That happened when an adult monitoring the tantalum mine through surveillance cameras noticed two robots not moving. The worker rushed in wearing a space suit and disconnected the robots—mine and Ingrid's—from each other. By then, of course, it was too late.

Ingrid had spoken to the world.

Here in the chamber, the lights grew brighter again. "Gentlemen," Vice Governor Patterson began, "I cannot presume all of you saw this yesterday when it broke live into all the major network programming. Even if you did see it then, or in subsequent newscasts, I want to remind you of the horror and abuse that is capable with robot control."

"I'm still not sure how all of it was broadcast," Vice Governor Armitage said. "The technology of this is far too confusing."

"We'll let Tyce Sanders answer."

They looked at me.

I swallowed. So far it didn't sound like they were going to vote in favor of robot control. But robot control wasn't the problem. It was the humans who took advantage of the technology and decided to abuse powerless people, like the 24 kids who were forced to operate the robots on the Moon.

"I can't explain exactly how it works," I said, "because I can't explain everything about how computers work. What I can tell you, though, is that I was able to reverse the information flow. Usually the robots give and take information to the brain. This time a bypass allowed Ingrid to send what she saw and heard through her robot circuits into mine. That was relayed to my computer on board the U.S. space station where I was and patched into a satellite feed."

In the tantalum mine, I'd made the connection from Ingrid's robot to my robot and then had immediately disengaged so I no longer controlled my robot. That turned my robot into a simple computer, and it continued to send information to our space station computer. Because Ms. Borris, before her disappearance, had been able to supply Dad with the codes that accessed the worldwide television network mainframe, it had been easy to hack into the network and feed the images to the entire world.

"I think I understand the basic concept," Vice Governor Michaels said after a few moments. His voice echoed in the quiet of the chamber. "And I would like to point out to my esteemed committee members that while this footage is an example of the horror possible with robot control, it is also an example of a problem solved by robot control."

Other vice governors nodded. This was good. I hoped.

"Furthermore," Michaels said, "I would like to draw your attention to the incident in Arizona."

Yes. Arizona. Where Cannon's commando group had been able to succeed in the relatively easy task of rescuing all the other kids outside the fortress.

"There," Michaels continued, "we have another example of the decisions made by adults that impact these children. From what I understand, the sergeant realized it was wrong to hold them captive and arranged to release them to a waiting rescue group."

Ha, I thought. The sergeant there just didn't want to let people know he thought he'd been haunted by a terrible singer and an old friend named Normie. But I would keep this secret.

"What are you saying?" Armitage asked.

Michaels answered. "Let's switch briefly to some more video I've asked to be made ready for this meeting."

The lights lowered. And there I was. Actually, there my robot was. Speaking to Ms. Borris in the interview.

"If there were 200 of you orbiting in space and all 200 of you controlled armed robots down here on Earth, wouldn't you be perfect soldiers? Don't you see potential danger in that?" she queried.

"Who would build the 200 armed robots? Who would put them in place?" I responded.

"I suppose it would be military people."

"Then maybe you should ask them those questions."

Immediately the lights brightened.

"It seems to me," Michaels said, "that this young man makes an excellent point. And let's not overlook the fact that he made it through the voice of a robot. It is still a human mind behind the robot. As he and the others grow older, they will still make decisions with their human minds. The robots are simply tools, like any other tools."

He paused. "And, yes, they can be weapons. Just as a simple kitchen knife can be used to cut bread or attack another person. My first point is this: there is nothing good or bad about the robots themselves. The issue we face is a much larger one. Controlling the intent of the people in power. And the events of the last few weeks, including the assassination attempt at the Summit of Governors, show that our children seem much more capable of doing what is right than some of those in power. More importantly, the power that the robots give them has allowed them to stop the very abuse the adults attempted."

Silence greeted that.

"My biggest concern," Michaels said, "is the possible damage to the children. They had no choice when they were operated on. Yet the operation is not possible on humans old enough to make the choice. Which means we must make a clear choice. Impose a worldwide ban on robot control and stop this technology or—"

"That would only drive it underground," Armitage objected. "Where only those with the power to abuse will have children who control robots. And I think we all know who I'm talking about."

Michaels smiled. "Exactly. Or we continue with robot control openly and embrace all the good that can come of it, while yet protecting ourselves and these children against the misuse of their persons and the technology. We need not look any further than the nuclear-plant incident to see how much this can help mankind. And then, of course, there is the Mars Project."

"I protest!" Vice Governor Calvin said sternly. "Look at

the young man in front of you. He is in a wheelchair. This was inflicted upon him without his consenting to the risk."

Michaels smiled again, calmly. "I agree. What I was going to propose is that every child who receives the operation is given the choice, when old enough, to continue with robot control or leave it. No child shall ever be forced to control robots."

"That is all very good," Calvin persisted, "but it doesn't address those children who suffer damage during surgery. If Tyce never wanted to control a robot again, he cannot go back to a normal life."

"Excellent point," Michaels countered. "I will address it two ways. First, his was the pioneer operation. Not only that, but it was done on Mars, without the proper equipment in case of an emergency. Since then, no other child has suffered damage. And second—" he paused and looked directly at me— "if damage is done to a child, all the resources available to us shall be used to help that individual child."

I wasn't sure I understood.

"What I propose is this," Michaels said to the others. "We form a set of guidelines that allow robot control to be used ethically and fairly. And guidelines that protect the welfare of the children involved in it. How many vote yes?"

All hands went up. Some slowly. Some quickly. But all went up.

"My second proposal, then, is part of the first. No matter

what the cost to us, we undo the harm that has been done to Tyce Sanders. And in the future to any other children."

My heart began to pound. Had I understood him correctly? But it couldn't be. There was no way the harm done to me could be reversed. I turned to look at my dad and was surprised to see tears in his eyes.

"Gentlemen," Michaels said to the rest of the chamber, "I have consulted extensively with medical experts over the last day. They tell me a successful operation on Tyce Sanders is possible. It will be difficult and very expensive, but it's possible. If we vote to allocate funds, Tyce Sanders may someday soon be able to walk."

Walk?

This time, all hands went up instantly.

Walk?

I finally understood.

Walk!

CHAPTER 25

04.08.2040

It took five hours after the ethics committee meeting for everything to settle down. I got tired of smiling for all the reporters afterward. To my surprise, all the vice governors voted *yes* to continuing robot control—as long as guidelines could be set to keep children from being abused, as they'd been in Arizona, in the Manchurian space station, and in the eight other pods of robot kids we'd discovered around the world.

I'm finally back in Dad's and my room at the Combat Force base outside New York City. I'm exhausted, yet somehow I can't sleep. Questions and answers keep running through my mind and mixing with each other.

As soon as Ingrid's live interview flashed across the world, Ms. Borris was released by the high-ranking military people. The barrage of information released to the world had uncloaked so much that they didn't dare press charges against her for breaking national security laws. She met Nate and me as soon as we stepped off our flight to New York. . . .

I was interrupted by a knock on the door. Dad had left a half hour ago to talk with Ms. Borris and the general. "Come on in." I had nothing to be afraid of now. Like there was any reason to lock your door at a military base anyway.

Ashley stepped in and quietly closed the door. She slumped into the chair next to me and kicked off her shoes. "Wow, am I tired."

That was the understatement of the world. "Yeah, me too."

"You know," she said softly, "it was nice—for at least a few hours—to be part of a real family . . . even if it seemed like it was difficult to fit in with those two who claimed to be my parents."

I nodded. It had taken a long time for me to feel like I knew my dad and that he was part of our family. Especially since over the years he had spent so much time away from us as a space pilot and . . .

My head still spun over Ms. Borris's words—that Dad was actually an agent for the U.S. military, fighting against the Terratakers. Boy, did we have a lot to talk about when he got back to the room. Some of the little things that had happened since we landed on Earth were now starting to make sense. It had all been a setup to protect Dad from being revealed as an agent within the U.S. division of the Combat Force.

I had so many questions. I yawned. If I could stay awake until he got back to the room that is . . .

"Tyce," Ashley jumped in, "are you really going to do it? think about having the operation where you could walk again?"

I was quiet for a couple of minutes. Finally I said the only thing I could. "I don't know. If it means I might lose the ability to control robots . . ."

"It's okay if you don't want to talk about it now," Ashley said quickly, with her eyes on the floor. "But I just wanted you to know that whatever you decide is okay with me."

With those few words she got up, picked up her shoes, and dangled them in her hands as she walked toward the door. "And, Tyce?" she said just before she stepped into the hallway. "You're the closest person to family I'll ever have."

Then, with the glitter of a tear in her eye and a flash of her silver cross earring, Ashley was gone.

I sat motionless, thinking and fingering the other silver cross she'd given me as a gift a long time ago, when she thought we might have to say good-bye for a long time. Then, slowly, my hands moved back to the keyboard.

Sometimes life just seems so unfair. Like how people can abuse kids by sticking them in jelly tubes and making them control robots without having a life. But even with things like that happening in the world, I've come to believe that God is still in control. People can use things for evil, but as Mom says, "God always intends things for good."

And she's right. There is no doubt now that the kids on the space station orbiting the Moon are going to be released. With all the public, worldwide pressure, the Manchurians have already released a press statement that the children will be let go as soon as transportation will allow it. Further, they claim to be horrified that one of their space stations was being used for such a purpose as child slavery. That is their claim. But one by one, other countries that once backed the Manchurians have begun to distance themselves from them.

In an effort to sway public opinion, the Manchurians have promised to launch a search via the children's DNA and all known hospital DNA records. They're also asking parents of missing children to supply blood samples for DNA testing, all in an effort to find the children's parents, matching the search that the Americans are doing for the kids in Arizona. The Manchurian promises might not be enough. On Earth, at least, the Manchurians look like they are on a downward slide.

As for linking the children with their parents, it will take a while. I'm just glad it worked out in Arizona as planned. But I would like to know why the general and the helicopter pilot . . .

I stopped keyboarding and let other questions flood into my mind. . . . What about Dr. Jordan and Luke Daab? They hadn't yet been located. Had they given up fighting for the Terratakers?

And the question that meant the most for the Earth's future: Would the theory of the carbon-dioxide generators speed along an atmosphere for Mars? Could it become inhabitable for humans outside the dome?

I sighed. All of these questions certainly weren't helping me to fall asleep.

Just then the door opened again. It was Dad, looking exhausted but happy. His tie hung crookedly against his shirt, which was open at the neck. I'd long ago shed my ethics committee attire for a comfortable Combat Force jumpsuit I'd found in the closet of our room.

"Information on the Moon pod was just released to the

public," Dad said. "And Chad, the general's son, is supposedly among the kids who will soon be shuttled to Earth. We're still waiting to see if the supreme governor's grandson comes up on the list too. He was kidnapped about the same time as Chad."

"Did you have a chance to ask Cannon about the helicopter pilot?"

Dad nodded. "We can talk more about that later. But remember the kind of pressure that was being put on Cannon. His own son was a hostage in the pod."

"Big pressure," I agreed.

"And remember that all of this has hinged on world public opinion. Cannon knew if the media finally exposed all of this, his son would be safe. But Cannon couldn't betray the military faction that wanted everything kept secret."

"With you so far. But that doesn't explain the helicopter pilot who tried to kill us, then shows up later in his office."

"The pilot didn't try to kill you. At Cannon's instructions, he made it look that way. Cannon was ready to take over the controls."

I didn't get it. "Cannon wanted it that way?"

"Remember the bomb in your wheelchair and that last-minute rescue? Ever wonder how they knew about the bomb? Cannon put it there. He set the whole thing up. He had to."

"Because . . . ?"

"It began to shift public opinion. He knew the hidden

Terratakers in the Combat Force would have no choice but to do everything possible to protect you. In short, he disarmed them, knowing they would have liked you out of the way."

I let out a deep breath. "But he couldn't ever tell me in case the listening devices were nearby."

"Exactly." Dad walked over to me and put a hand on my shoulder. "Tyce, I'm really proud of you. For going ahead with the mission to help the kids, even without me. For everything you're doing with the robots. For appearing before the ethics committee . . ."

He tousled my hair. Less than a year ago, when I didn't like him very much, I would have hated that. Now I didn't mind.

"Thanks, Dad," I said. Then I grinned. "Don't you think it's about time to do what I told the robots in the tantalum mine? 'Time to go home'?"

"You bet," he said enthusiastically.

It *was* time. Time for us to go back to our *real* home. A place with a butterscotch sky and blue sun.

Mars.

And I couldn't wait. . . .

JOURNAL
TWO

CHAPTER 1

Tidal wave!

Not water. But blood. Whooshing down a narrow pipeline.

I knew the rush of blood was out there only because I could hear it surge ahead with each heartbeat—a sound like a distant drum. But I couldn't see anything because I was inside a shiny steel transporter pod, half the size of a pea, carried along by the powerful flow of blood.

Well, actually, it wasn't me inside the pod but the miniature robot I controlled through virtual reality. But it *felt* like I was inside the pod. Since my brain waves were connected to the robot, I saw and heard what the robot saw and heard. In turn, the robot responded to my brain waves and moved the way my own body would move.

The robot itself was an incredible piece of machinery. It was a second-generation ant-bot, about one-tenth the size of the original mini-robots. And those first ones were smaller than an ant!

Yet even being that tiny, there wasn't much room for the robot's arms and legs to move in the absolute darkness of the pod. There certainly was nothing to see inside. All I could do was wait and listen to the blood outside as the transporter pod moved through the major arteries of the president of the United States of America.

Inside the operating room, the president sat calmly in a chair, hooked to heartbeat monitors, waiting for the transporter pod to reach the pacemaker in her heart. Something had caused it to slow down, and the doctors didn't know what. Checking it by robot was much easier on her than having a major operation that would open her chest cavity and keep her in the hospital for weeks.

Just a few minutes earlier, a doctor had injected the tiny pod into an artery in her hip. A beeping locator signal let the doctor know of its progress. As my robot waited, the doctor guided the pod through the president's arteries with a powerful magnet. The inside of the pod was lined with a thin rubber coating so the electrical forces generated by the magnet wouldn't disturb the intricate wiring of the robot. But the X-ray signals could still get through the rubber, and that allowed me to stay in contact with the doctor.

"Tyce," the doctor said, "you're moving toward the lungs now. I'm sorry it's taking so long, but I made a wrong turn at the kidneys. After all, this is the first time something like this has ever been tried."

Although I couldn't see anything, I imagined the walls of the arteries stretching and throbbing with each beat of the heart. I imagined glowing red saucer-shaped platelets swarming just outside my pod.

"Tyce," the doctor continued, "are you ready? I mean, really ready? We're talking about a human life at stake. And this human happens to be the president of the most powerful country in the world. If she dies, a lot of other people will suffer."

"Yes, sir," I said. "I'm ready."

The doctor had explained it to me earlier. When the pod reached the right place near the president's heart, he would trigger the pod to release some tiny spikes that would secure it to the blood vessel. Then the pod would open, and my robot would seek its target—the president's pacemaker.

I'd spent hours going over the model of a pacemaker, studying computer-generated images to give me an understanding of how it would appear to my little robot.

"I'm ready," I confirmed. "As soon as the pod opens."

It took the doctor another 30 seconds. "Get ready," he warned.

"Ready," I repeated.

And blood rushed in as the pod cracked open.

Immediately my robot began to sway with the movement of the blood. The president's heartbeat had fallen to 30 beats per minute. One every two seconds. A hard tidal wave rushed over me; then it became relatively calm and I floated in an ebb of blood.

A beat every two seconds. Slower than if she'd been asleep. Her heart wasn't pumping enough blood, and her body desperately needed oxygen. Already some of her major organs had begun to shut down.

My robot was tethered to the inside of the transporter pod by a microscopic strand of titanium. The next heartbeat would pump blood that would shoot me forward until I reached the end of it, like a dog running to the end of its leash.

A light attached to the robot's right arm showed a red glow of blood around it. But if the doctor had placed the pod correctly, the next heartbeat would take me right into the pacemaker and . . .

The robot shot forward as blood gushed again through the artery. Then it stopped hard. I'd hit the pacemaker!

Now my tiny light bounced off the shininess of the pace-maker's plastic. It would have to be enough.

The light showed a small seam. I grabbed it and held on. I needed to be secure before the next heartbeat washed a new wave of blood over me.

The wave came. It tugged at my robot body.

I held.

I climbed farther for another second.

I held. Waited for another rush of blood. Then climbed.

Again and again. Until finally I reached a small opening that led into the pacemaker.

I waited for another heartbeat to pass before moving inside.

Once inside, I needed to find a wire that, although nearly invisible to human eyes, would look like a thick rope to a robot this size. The wire sent an electrical current to the pacemaker controls from its power source. It was insulated, so I didn't have to worry about putting my robot in risk of shock, which could also shock my own brain. It was this wire that doctors suspected was loose or frayed, causing the slower heartbeat.

My robot hand finally found the wire. It was so big in comparison that I could barely wrap the robot fingers around it. I grabbed and held tight.

That was my mistake. I should have been holding something else.

The next wave of blood shifted my robot body.

I forgot to let go of the wire.

It held me briefly, then snapped loose as blood tugged at my robot body. For a moment my robot body swayed. Then it stopped, suspended in blood.

And I realized what had happened. I'd disconnected the

wire that, until then, had just been frayed or loose. All heart-beats of the pacemaker stopped.

"Tyce!" the doctor shouted. "What's going on in there? The president is screaming with pain. She has—!" He stopped for a second, then shouted louder, "Tyce! She's collapsed. We can't get a heartbeat on these monitors! Tyce! Tyce Sanders! Do something in there!"

CHAPTER 2

"Can you scratch my back?" I begged Ashley. A cast covered my body from my knees all the way up to just below my armpits. The skin beneath my body cast was so itchy I wouldn't have cared if she used a chain saw to get at it.

I'd just finished my virtual-reality simulation, and my heart was still pounding.

"You just killed the first woman president in the history of the United States, and that's the first thing you're going to say for history to record?" Ashley exclaimed, helping me take off my sensory-deprivation helmet.

I rubbed my face where the helmet had pressed for the last half hour. The helmet was designed to make sure no light or sound reached my own eyes or ears during robot control. Even though it was tight enough to be barely comfortable, it was an improvement on the headset and blindfold I had first used to go into robot control.

Of course, with the total backing of the World United Federation after uncovering the plot to kill the vice governors, all of our stuff had been replaced with the best and newest equipment. This included updated computer programs to simulate situations where robot control could help the rest of humankind. Things like robot submarines. Robot helicopters. Robot firefighters. And robot surgical units, like the ones used in the virtual-reality medical emergency I had just failed.

I knew a little about the history of computers and how this new ant-bot was technologically possible. The first silicon computer chips—way, way back in the late 1900s—were wafers hardly bigger than a pinkie fingernail. Now those wafers looked like baseball stadiums compared to the modern computer chips, which were tinier than a pinhead. Information pathways were etched on these chips less than a molecule in width. My small robot needed only two chips for all its computing work, and the robot's arms and legs were so tiny that only other miniature robots—guided by human brains—could build them.

Ashley floated beside me, holding my helmet by its strap. She had just unhooked me from my robot-control transmitter. "At least I was almost able to fix her pacemaker," she said, rubbing in her own success. Her dark almond-shaped eyes crinkled as she grinned. "Every time *you* tried, the blood knocked you out of your pod."

Okay, so she had me there. Ashley was right. She was a good match for me in virtual-reality skills. Although I wouldn't tell her so outright, secretly I was glad. After all, that was what had brought us together as friends when she'd arrived on the planet of Mars almost four years ago.

During the past two and a half years on Earth, as we waited for the orbit rotation of Earth and Mars to line up so that my dad could take us back to Mars, Ashley and I had become even closer. It isn't just any friend who hangs around when you have to spend most of your time visiting doctors and having multiple tests—or when you're up to your eyeballs in a cast. After saving the vice governors' lives, I'd been told it was possible I would be able to walk again. But it could mean losing my ability to control robots through virtual reality.

It sounds crazy, I know, but the choice had been tough. I'd never been able to walk my whole life—but my world, and all my training since I was a kid, had been in virtual reality. It was hard to think about giving that up.

But after a lot of discussions with my dad, my mom, and Rawling, I'd decided to go for it. And Ashley had been my biggest supporter, keeping my mind busy—especially over the two months I'd spent in the body cast on Earth and now these almost six months on the spaceship back to Mars.

It was Ashley who had insisted that I try connecting

with a robot soon into my recovery after surgery. I'd been too scared to try it by myself. And I'd been surprised—and greatly relieved—when my spinal plug still worked to connect my brain waves to a robot. So at least I knew that part of my life would still work.

But could I walk? Actually be able to take steps on my own, outside of virtual reality with a robot? It had been eight months since my surgery, and I still had to wait and see.

I was glad Ashley was still by my side . . . and that she still had her sense of humor. As annoying as it could be sometimes.

I wrinkled my nose at her, knowing that my small action would speak louder than words.

"There's always tomorrow," Ashley teased, attempting to tuck a strand of her straight, shoulder-length black hair behind her ear. "Give me one more try and—"

I sucked in a breath at the itchiness of my ribs. If only there were room to squeeze my hands inside the cast and scratch, scratch, scratch with my fingernails. Until I'd been put in this body cast, I'd spent my life in a wheel-chair. But I'd never once dreamed there would come a day when I'd think a wheelchair was freedom. Yet compared to the prison of this cast, I wondered. . . . Tubes seemed to stick out of me everywhere. The ones I hated the most were those that fed my body wastes into a pouch hidden by my jumpsuit pants.

"This close to Mars," I answered, "we should probably spend more time on the carbon-dioxide generators."

I didn't mean that she or I should hook up to a carbon-dioxide machine, of course. After all, we humans breathe oxygen. But the atmosphere on Mars needed more carbon dioxide, and that's why we were on our way.

We meaning 50 kids like Ashley and me who had robot-control capability. After hearing about the need for human life to expand to new planets like Mars and the capabilities of the new carbon-dioxide generators to provide an atmosphere in which life could thrive, 50 of the kids had also decided to come—on their own. They were excited about being part of "saving the Earth" in a unique way—by controlling the robots that worked the carbon-dioxide generators.

And now within two days we'd land on the red planet. After a trip of 50 million miles.

But before we did, we all needed as much virtual-reality practice as possible assembling the parts to the carbon-dioxide generators. On Mars we would be building the real giant gas generators on the surface of the planet.

"I can't give up on this pacemaker thing," Ashley said. "One of us has got to be able to save her life one of these times. Poor woman must be tired of dying."

The poor woman wasn't real—just a computer model. And one of the many different programs the World United Federation had created for the Mars journey. I couldn't imagine how many millions and millions of dollars had been spent to generate the programs since the technology first became public. But with 50 of us spending six months in space traveling from Earth to Mars, we needed something to do that could be of good use down the road.

Although the stuff we did to pass time was practical, it didn't feel like work. The virtual-reality simulation programs were fun and good training, and we had plenty of time to read books. Ashley liked fiction; I was really getting into science. Learning about . . .

Ashley poked me. I was spacing out again, mentally writing in my journal. I'd first hated it—when my mom had made me start it as homework almost four years ago on Mars. But now I used it to track my thoughts and think through problems.

"She might be tired of dying in virtual reality," I said, "but here in real life I'm dying to get scratched. Can't you find anything to help?"

Ashley raised an eyebrow and put her hand on her hip in her trademark gesture. "Just another powder injection."

"A wire," I begged. "A stick with sandpaper on the end. Something to rub my skin."

"Powder," she insisted. "I'm your friend and you have strict doctors' orders not to use anything but powder. Scratching skin beneath a cast can lead to sores and infections and scars."

"Powder, then." I made a face. Ever since I'd been in the body cast I'd needed someone to inject a special medical powder beneath my cast twice a day. It helped keep my skin dry and also had a numbing effect to get rid of the itching as my body healed from the surgery. But I really, really wanted the feeling of something to scratch at the skin. In one way, it would be great to get out of the cast.

And in another way, I was worried about the day the cast was taken off because if—

I stopped my thoughts. I was too afraid to wonder what would happen then.

"You all right?" Ashley asked, catching the expression on my face. It was hard to fool her.

I grunted, "Fine." Then a sudden headache hit me so hard it felt like a hand grenade had just exploded inside my brain.

Ashley put the helmet in my hand and pushed away. In the weightlessness of outer space, that effort moved her easily toward the hatchway that led out of the computer room to the rest of the spaceship.

She stopped at the hatchway. "Could be worse, you know," she said, looking at me intently. "If you have to be in a body cast, at least it's in a zero-gravity situation."

That's the way the doctors had planned it. Zero gravity meant I could still be mobile. More important, it would give my spinal cord the best situation to repair the nerve splinting they had done. So they'd done my surgery only two months before I left Earth—enough time for them to make sure there were no complications but not enough time for me to go crazy in Earth's atmosphere.

"You're right." I tried to smile through the incredible headache that gripped my skull. I should have expected it. These headaches were coming like clockwork, once every four hours. They were lasting longer and longer, some for 10 minutes. Was there something wrong inside my brain? I was scared to even mention them to anyone—much less Ashley or my dad, who would really be worried.

As I spoke to Ashley, I continued to smile to hide the pain. "It could be worse."

But not much. I'd had little headaches before on Mars and on Earth. Ones that were dull and just annoying. But these headaches were different. They'd only begun a few months earlier, halfway through the trip to Mars. Every day they were becoming more and more intense. I wondered if they would kill me before our fleet of spaceships reached Mars.

And that was only two days away.

CHAPTER 3

The red planet filled much of the view from the observatory. I couldn't believe I'd be home soon. My years on Earth had been so full of adventure that sometimes Mars hadn't seemed real. Only the memories of my mom and Rawling were still vivid.

Funny though, how the more a person does in life, the more it brings good-byes. Good-bye when leaving Mars, then good-bye to friends when leaving Earth. I felt torn between two homes. Back on Earth, it hadn't been easy saying good-bye to my friends Cannon and Nate. And I could tell from the other kids' tears when saying good-bye to their parents that they felt the same. Chad had changed his mind at the last minute and stayed with his dad, the general who had helped us on Earth. It was the same with the supreme governor's grandson, whom Ashley and I had rescued from robot-control slavery.

But what choice did a person have? If baby birds never left the nest, they never learned to fly. All of us had a destiny to follow and . . .

"Science book in your lap but eyes closed and daydreaming, huh?"

I opened my eyes. "Uh, hi, Ashley."

"Learning anything?"

"The usual."

"More science?"

"It's interesting," I said.

"Right."

"Okay, then," I said. "How bright would it seem to you if you were standing in the center of the sun?"

Although there were other kids on board the ship, she and I were alone in the ship's observatory.

Three hours had passed since I'd wrecked the virtual pacemaker of the virtual president of the United States. My headache was gone. My skin didn't itch quite so bad. And I was floating beneath the eyepiece of a telescope that extended through the upper panels of the spaceship.

It wasn't until I'd spent time on Earth that I realized outer space allowed such an incredibly clear view of the stars and galaxies. On Earth, stars twinkled as the atmosphere bent their light; here in space, the stars were bright enough against a black background to hurt the eyes.

I grinned and shook my head. Sometimes I could be so stubborn. . . .

"Huh?" Ashley's face was buried in her comp-board.

"If you were standing in the center of the sun, how bright would it be?" I said again.

Ashley looked up from her homework. "Answering that beats trying to figure out Shakespeare. And I know it's a trick question. You wouldn't see a thing. You'd be burned to a crisp. Just like what nearly happened to us on the trip to Earth because of Luke Daab."

Luke Daab . . . the very name made me shiver. Who would think such a mousy-looking guy could cause such big trouble?

"It's not a trick question," I said, swinging the telescope idly in different directions. "If you could survive in the middle of the sun, how bright would it be on your eyes?"

She paused her keyboarding.

I kept scanning outer space. I blinked as a large, dark object seemed to jump into view. It was another spaceship in our fleet, its circular shape gleaming dully because of light from the sun a couple hundred million miles away. Including manned and unmanned supply vehicles, there were 10 space-ships altogether. All of us were at least 1,000 miles apart— above, below, and to the sides—cruising through the frictionless vacuum of space at 15,000 miles an hour. To assemble this fleet, the expense for Earth had been a huge gamble. But if it paid off, it would change history. And save billions of lives because it would open up a new planet for human inhabitation.

"I want to say it would be dark," Ashley said, her dark eyes squinting in thought. "Just because you wouldn't ask the question unless it had some kind of weird answer. But on the other hand, maybe you're trying a reverse on me, and you'll laugh if I don't give the obvious answer."

"What's your guess then?" I smirked.

"Dark," she said at first. Then, more emphatically, "No. Bright. I have to go with bright. So bright you couldn't stand it. I mean, the sun's a couple of million degrees. That kind of heat *has* to be bright."

"It's 27 million degrees in the center, 4.5 million degrees halfway to the surface, and only 10,000 degrees on the surface," I said without looking up from the telescope. "That's in Fahrenheit. If you want it in Celsius, the temperatures are—"

"Remind me never to get stuck in a body cast. If all you do is fill your head with useless facts, then—"

I must have looked strange to her. To cover my body cast, I wore an extra-large jumpsuit. My legs stuck straight out, unable to move. And I was just floating underneath the eyepiece, my entire body rigid and straight.

I interrupted her right back. "And even with that kind of heat, the sun is pitch-black in the center. It would be darker to you than in the darkest cave in the middle of the Earth. No light at all would reach your eyes."

I finally looked away from my telescope and at Ashley. She was smiling.

"Okay, you've got me curious," she said. "Why is the center of the sun that dark?"

"First of all, you have to realize how big the sun is," I answered. "Over three-quarters of a million miles across. A person your size weighs about 100 pounds on Earth. On the sun, its force of gravity would make you weigh over two tons."

Her eyes widened in surprise. "Wow! Tyce, something amazing—"

I waved away her awe at my knowledge. "Keep thinking about that gravity. You see, gravity packs all of the atoms of the sun so tightly together that the rays of light don't get a chance to become rays of light. It's like a—"

"Tyce, you don't understand! I think I—"

"Listen to the professor," I said grandly, continuing my lecture. "Think of a big bag jammed with marbles and a little peewee marble trying to squeeze through. That's what an energy ray has to do as it moves away from the center of the sun. The ray bounces from atom to atom as it heads toward the cooler surface. It makes no light. Isn't it cool? Science has shown that all of the physics laws were predetermined even before the universe began and—"

"Tyce!"

Again I ignored her interruption. Science was fascinating, and I was determined to finish my little story for her.

"Getting back to the sun, it takes 100,000 years for a ray to escape the center and reach the edge and finally become a light ray. Then, finally free of the interference of those tightly packed atoms, it zooms to 186,000 miles per second, flashes through space, and in less than nine minutes, travels the 93 million miles to Earth. After waiting 100,000 years to emerge."

Lying motionless in midair, I folded my arms across my chest. "What do you think about that?"

"Interesting," Ashley said in an almost detached tone. I stopped thinking and focused on her. Her eyes were still wide and she was staring at me. "But not as interesting as the end of your right foot."

"Huh?"

She pointed. "Your right foot. While you were talking, I noticed it. That's what I was trying to tell you."

"Is this some sort of trick? To change the subject or something?" I began.

"No," she said. Then a tear rolled down her cheek. "It's not a trick at all."

"I don't get it," I said, suddenly scared. I hadn't had much experience with girls beyond my friendship with Ashley. But I knew enough to realize it's not good when girls start to cry. "What did I do wrong? Is my foot too smelly for you? Is that why you noticed it?"

She began to laugh but kept crying at the same time.

"Your toes. Under the sock of your jumpsuit, I saw your toes move while you were talking."

Toes? Move? I lifted my head and looked down my body. I could see the top of my toes. I watched them closely. *Wiggle,* I commanded my toes. *Wiggle.*

I'd tried that thousands of times growing up. Sitting in my wheelchair, I'd stare at my leg or my foot or my toes and try to move them by concentrating hard. I'd prayed. I'd begged God to let them move. Until years of disappointment convinced me otherwise, I believed that—just once—I could think hard enough to send my lower body a message. To make it listen to me. Or that God would do a miracle and *poof!* I'd be able to walk again.

But nothing had ever happened. Not for a kid whose spinal cord had been damaged when he was barely more than a baby. That was probably one reason it had taken me so long to believe that God not only existed, but he really cared about me.

Except now my toes moved. Just a little. *But they moved!*

"Oh, wow," I said.

Ashley pushed off a wall in my direction. When she reached me, she gave me a hug. "They did move, didn't they?" she said between a few more tears and giggles.

"Oh, wow," I repeated. And then I began to cry too.

That's how we were when the intercom buzzed. Hugging and crying and laughing.

"Hello?" Ashley said, wiping away her tears.

"Tyce and Ashley . . ." It was my dad, the fleet's lead pilot. "Thought I'd find you there," he said. "Look, I need you in the navigation cone. Immediately."

CHAPTER 4

Dad was waiting for us in the navigation cone of our spaceship.

This ship had an identical design to all the other manned ships of the fleet. And while it was new, it was similar to the design of the *Moon Racer,* the shuttle that had taken us to Earth from Mars years earlier.

The navigation cone formed the nose of the ship and had a great view. The bulk of the ship, made of a titanium-steel alloy, lay behind it. For maximum protection and less expense, the bunks and work areas had no windows. These rooms were lit by the pale whiteness of low-energy argon tubes set into the walls.

Essentially, the entire ship was a large circular tube, moving sideways through the vacuum of space. The outer part of this large tube held the docking port, two emergency escape pods, an exercise room, all the passenger bunks, and work-area compartments. The inner part of the circle formed a corridor, which we traveled by grabbing handholds and pushing forward or backward, entering the bunks or work areas through circular hatches with slide-away covers. Also from this corridor, four main hatches led to tubes that extended downward like spokes. They met at a hub in the center so that the four tubes formed an X in the center of the giant circle. From the hub at the center where they connected, one short tube led backward to the pyramid-shaped ion-drive engine. Another short tube led forward to this pyramid-shaped navigation cone.

Here the titanium structure of the rest of the ship had been replaced by material that looked and functioned like glass but was thousands of times stronger and more expensive. All the walls of the pyramid were made of this space glass, including the floor. The computer and control console sat on this glass floor, as did the pilot's seat. That's why I liked it so much. Pushing from the hub into the navigation cone made it seem like a person was floating directly into clear outer space. This sensation frightened some people, but because in gravity situations I had spent so much time in a wheelchair, I loved the feeling of freedom.

There was something so awesome about staring into the infinite world of deep space. For me, it always brought more questions about how the matter had come to be in the first place. And more importantly, why? These were God questions. And I still had so many others that I would love to ask him directly. Sitting in the navigation cone always brought those questions back.

Normally I would have pushed into the cone and pressed up against the space glass and stared at Mars. When the sun was on it, it was a beautiful red globe, growing slightly larger each day.

Mars—my home.

But for the moment, I hardly noticed it.

My dad sat in the pilot's seat in front of the control console. He turned as Ashley and I pushed through the hatch into the navigation cone.

Letting our momentum carry us forward, we floated toward him.

People say I look like him—even more so as I've grown older. I have the same dark blond hair he does. My nose and jaw and forehead were still bigger than I wanted them to be, but the rest of my face was starting to catch up. He was big, square and rugged like a football player. It would be great if I kept growing and became his size too. Of course, that's assuming when I got out of my body cast that . . .

I thought of my toes. How they had wiggled. And I wished this were the time to tell Dad. But his face was set in a frown. I'd save it for later.

"Dad," I said, "we got here as quickly as we could."

He nodded but seemed distracted. He pointed at his computer screen. "I've got something you need to see."

Dad didn't move from in front of the screen to give us a better look. He didn't have to. Not in zero gravity. I hung upside down, above the screen. Ashley stretched horizontally behind him, looking over his shoulder.

Each of the spaceships in the fleet sent positioning signals to all the others. On the computer screen, each was a tiny white blip. If I had taken out a pen and connected the outer blips of the formation, I would have drawn a perfect diamond almost filling the screen. Since Dad was the lead pilot, our ship was at the front, with the others in formation behind. Ten ships, moving majestically and silently in space, thousands of miles apart. Some, like this one, held passengers. The others transported supplies and disassembled carbon-dioxide generators.

"The pattern seems normal to me," I told Dad. I'd been worried there was trouble with one of the spaceships. Even though the former Manchurian military superpower had lost a series of battles during my Earth years, the World United Federation feared that their Terrataker rebels might try to stop our fleet as a last chance to win their war against the rest of the world.

"It is normal. But watch this." Dad repeatedly punched a button on the console. The computer screen shifted and zoomed out. Again and again. Where once the diamond formation had filled the whole screen, it was reduced to half the screen. Then a quarter. It kept getting smaller and smaller until the blips of all 10 ships merged into one large blip.

Dad shrunk the screen more, and that large blip became almost invisible. Since it was plotted on a computer map of the solar system, the background was studded with the lights of brighter stars.

"Now it's like seeing our space fleet from millions of miles away, right?" I asked.

"Essentially yes, although you need to keep in mind it's a computer simulation of roughly 20 million miles of space. If the scale was truly accurate, you wouldn't even see the blip that represents our fleet." As Dad spoke, he tried to look straight up into my face. He grimaced as his neck twisted. "Let me get you down here on Ashley's level."

He was belted into the chair, so it took him very little effort to pull me beside him and spin my legs back so I was horizontal beside Ashley. My face was on one side of his shoulder. Hers on the other.

He glanced back and forth between Ashley and me. "Keep in mind that our formation is on the right-hand side of the screen, almost at Mars. Now look at the left side of the screen."

"If the scale is 20 million miles," Ashley said, "wouldn't that be about halfway back to Earth?"

"Pretty close," Dad said. He almost touched the screen as he pointed to a star.

Except it wasn't a single star.

"Watch closely again," he said as he hit the console button a few more times. The screen began to zoom in, each time making the white blip bigger. Seconds later the blip began to transform into an entire formation of blips.

"Looks like another fleet of spaceships," I joked. "Weird that from this angle the stars would seem to fit together that way."

"Tyce," Dad said quietly, "it *is* another space fleet."

"What?"

"I've received notice from the World United Federation. Our biggest fear has come true. It's a fleet sent by the Manchurians."

I shuddered. "Are you sure?"

"Take a look at the style of the ships," Dad replied. He clicked and clicked to zoom in closer. "See those markings?"

Ashley and I both looked closer, almost bumping our heads together.

"I believe," Dad said, "they intend to invade Mars."

CHAPTER 5

That night, as usual in zero gravity, I hooked my belt to my sleeping bunk so I wouldn't push off accidentally during the night and float into one of the opposite walls of my room.

I closed my eyes. But I doubted I would fall asleep. Too many thoughts bounced through my head.

If the next headache arrived on schedule, it wouldn't be for another two hours. I was glad for the chance to think without pain. I tried to direct my thoughts toward the Manchurian invasion.

Writing always helped me think, so I began to keyboard a journal entry.

The key now for the Manchurians is to somehow take control of Mars. If they have it, they have leverage against all the other countries in the world. And control now is more important than ever, because it looks like the carbon-dioxide generators the space fleet carries will make it possible for Mars to become a colony in 10 years, instead of the 100 years that had first been projected.

I stopped keyboarding and stared blankly at my computer screen. The Manchurian space fleet should have worried me as I lay floating in the darkness, trying to fall asleep. The Terratakers had been doing everything possible to take over the Mars Project. If the Manchurians were on their way, I had no doubt that it meant Dr. Jordan and Luke Daab were with them.

However, my thoughts kept moving away to something else. I was too selfish. All I could think about was my toes. How they had wiggled at my command.

It's so easy to take your body for granted. I was just as guilty of this as anyone. In my wheelchair growing up, I was still able to move my arms and hands and head. I never gave much thought to how incredible that was. Your brain sends a command to your hands, and they move. Sometimes I forgot about the miracle of that because I got mad that my legs wouldn't respond. Those were the times that God seemed far away—or rather, the times that I didn't want to talk to him. I was mad at him too, so I ignored him. Pretended he wasn't there at all. Then a bunch of crises in my life and under the dome had forced me to think about him and discover who he really was. That there was more to life than what we saw on the surface. So I had come to peace, and it was easier to accept how he'd made me unique—even if it meant I was in a wheelchair for life.

And now, for the first time I could remember, my toes had moved!

After my surgery, the doctors had refused to make promises. They had said only time would tell if the surgery would work. But if my toes had moved after all these months in a body cast in space . . .

Lying in the darkness, I began to swell with hope. Maybe when the cast came off, I would be able to walk. To run! *What would it feel like?* I wondered.

Just as I began to daydream about running through the dome and catching a football thrown to me by Ashley, our ship exploded.

At least that's what it felt like to me.

It took a second to realize the explosion had happened in my head. The headache had arrived early. Even though my eyes were closed in agony, I saw flashing lights and stars, the way it is when you hit your head against something.

And just when I couldn't stand the pain any longer, the flashing lights shut down into total blackness.

CHAPTER 6

I met Dad at breakfast.

Well, it wasn't actually breakfast. Just some liquids in plastic bags called nutrient-tubes. I drank carefully for two reasons. First, although I had woken up normally when the alarm on my watch sounded, my head still throbbed a little. And second, you don't want to spill anything in zero gravity.

Once Ashley had told me a joke while I was sucking orange juice. I'd laughed and some of the orange juice had gone down the wrong throat tube. Because of my coughing fit, I'd spewed orange juice in all directions.

On Earth that would only mean a sticky mess on the floor, easy to clean up with a couple of wipes.

In zero gravity? Hundreds of tiny orange-juice pellets had immediately spread through the eating room. It had

taken 10 minutes to chase them all down, slurping each one
back into my mouth as Ashley groaned in disgust.

This morning I was alone in the eating room until Dad
pushed through the hatch, holding a folded piece of paper.
"Hey," he said, "Ashley tells me you have some news. Hope
it's good. I could use some right about now."

I gave Dad the best smile I could. "My toes wiggled last
night. I didn't say anything because the Manchurian fleet . . ."

"Sidetracked us," Dad finished for me, worry spreading
across his face. Then his eyes grew wide, as if he'd just realized what I'd said. "Really?" he said slowly. "Your toes actually wiggled? Let's see."

I looked down and focused. They moved again. And even
more than last time.

"I can hardly wait to tell your mother!" Dad exclaimed,
grinning broadly.

"Me too," I said.

Then Dad's grin faded. "You all right? I thought you'd be
a little more excited."

"Just worried about the other ships," I said, trying to act
as nonchalant as possible. I didn't want to concern him further by telling him about my headaches.

Dad nodded and held up the piece of paper. "The other
fleet. With all that's happened since you left Mars, I don't
blame you for thinking the worst."

It was my turn to nod. If he thought I was worried about

the Manchurians, I was going to leave it that way. He had enough to think about as head pilot of the fleet with people like Jordan and Daab on our tail. I'd keep my headaches to myself. Especially since I doubted there was anything he—or anyone else on board the spaceship—could do about them.

"This isn't going to make you any happier either," Dad said. He handed me the paper. "A printout from Rawling."

What kind of bad news would Rawling send? I wondered.

I unfolded the paper. It was an e-mail.

From: "Rawling McTigre" <mctigrer@marsdome.ss>
To: "Chase Sanders" <sandersc@marsdome.ss>
Sent: 04.24.2043, 2:39 P.M.
Subject: Manchurian fleet

Chase (and Tyce),
    Last night I received from Earth the same computer information that they indicated was sent to you. I presume you downloaded it immediately and saw that the Manchurian fleet is only a couple of months behind.
    My director's report contains some additional information—that military officials on Earth just learned about the fleet themselves. Evidently the Manchurians assembled their own fleet on the dark side of the Moon and launched it in secrecy.

So that explains it, I thought. Why no one—not even the higher-ups on Earth—seemed to know about the fleet until now.

Rawling's e-mail went on:

However, don't worry. Because you'll be arriving first, we should have ample time to set up the surface-to-space missile system you are bringing with you.

See you in two days. Stay in touch—and God bless your journey!

Rawling

P.S. In the meantime, Kristy sends you and Tyce and Ashley all her love. She can't wait to see you!

Kristy. My mom. I was glad to know Mom was thinking about me, just like I was thinking about her. When I didn't have to worry about killer headaches and a killer Manchurian fleet, of course.

"I don't get it," I said, reading the e-mail twice. "It was well publicized that our fleet was carrying atomic missiles—in fact, enough to repel more than 10 Manchurian fleets—to protect Mars against future invasions. The whole point was to make sure the Manchurians didn't even try. So what do they think they can accomplish?"

"Rawling will give us all the information we're cleared to receive when we get to Mars," Dad said. He squeezed my shoulder lightly. "And just so you'll relax, Rawling has a good point. We do have a lot of time to set up our defenses before the other ships arrive."

"Maybe they have long-range weapons on their space-ships," I put in. I'd learned from experience that you never knew what the rebels were up to. "Maybe they'll nuke the dome before our weapons can nuke them."

"Maybe," Dad said quietly.

I studied his face. "You don't look worried."

"Ever since the Mars Dome was established 18 years ago, it hasn't needed weapons to protect itself from outer-space invasion. So tell me why Mars is suddenly considered valuable enough to be attacked."

"The carbon-dioxide generators," I said. It was an easy answer. That was the whole purpose of the fleet. Carbon dioxide meant that plants could grow. Growing plants produced oxygen. Eventually Mars would have enough atmosphere to be a new colony. And that means the colonization of Mars can take place that much faster.

"Exactly. If the Manchurians fire atomic weapons on Mars, it will destroy the very thing they want. So they won't. The only way Mars is worth anything to them is if they can land and take over the dome intact. But there's no way they can land once our surface-to-space missile system is in place. And we've got plenty of time to get it ready." Dad patted my leg. "No worries, then, right?"

I hardly heard him.

"Tyce? Tyce?"

I was staring at my left leg. The one he had just patted.

"Tyce?" he asked one more time.

I looked up at my dad, hardly daring to believe. "It's the strangest thing. I think I felt that."

"I'm not sure what you're talking about."

"The bottom of my leg. Where you touched me."

"Here?" Dad grabbed my calf and squeezed.

It felt like electricity running through my body—good, tingling electricity. "Yes! There!" I'd never felt any sensation in my legs before!

Dad high-fived me. Except we slapped palms so hard that it drove us apart in the zero gravity. Seconds later, Dad banged into one wall. I banged into another.

And all we did was grin at each other.

If only the chance to walk was all I had to worry about in the next few months. . . .

CHAPTER 7

That night, on the final hours before our approach to Mars, I was alone in the navigation cone, watching the planet loom closer and closer. I'd be back on the red planet within 24 hours.

Dad and everyone else on the spaceship were asleep. That meant the ship was on autopilot, so I had the navigation cone to myself.

I should have been asleep too, but another killer headache had struck. Not bad enough to knock me out this time, which would have been a mercy. Instead it had throbbed for about a half hour, leaving me dizzy and unable to sleep.

Usually in my quiet hours I wrote in my journal on my comp-board. So I had taken it to the navigation cone with me.

I had written a little.

I had dimmed all the lights and stared out into space. Through the glass it felt like I could reach out and touch Mars. And what a glorious sight! I was finally almost home—after a long three years.

Rawling had reported a huge dust storm, and it was just settling. As light from the sun behind the spaceship hit the planet at the right angle, I watched the horizon of Mars spin into sight.

It brought me Mount Olympus, its huge extinct crater sticking out of the dust storm. The mountain itself was bigger than Colorado and reached 15 miles into the sky.

I kept watching, without feeling sleepy at all.

The beauty made me sad, in a way. Because I wondered if there was a tumor or something in my brain to cause these headaches. Was I going to die? Would this be the last time I'd see something as incredible as Mars with the sun warming it?

To take my mind off my thoughts, I turned to my comp-board. But instead of writing, I found myself reading the first entry I had ever put in my journal. It brought back a lot of memories, reminding me of how I'd first learned of my robot-control abilities.

First, today's date: AD 06.20.2039, Earth calendar. It's been a little more than 14 years since the dome was established in 2025. When I think about it, that means some of the scientists and techies in the dome were my age around the year 2000, even though the last millennium seems like ancient history. Of course, kids back then didn't have to deal with water shortage wars and . . . an exploding population that meant we had to find a way to colonize Mars.

Things have become so desperate on Earth that already 500 billion dollars have been spent on this project, which seems like a lot until you do the math and realize that's only about 10 dollars for every person on the planet.

Kristy Sanders, my mom, used to be Kristy Wallace until she married my father, Chase Sanders. They teamed up with nearly 200 men and women specialists from all countries across the world when the first ships left Earth. I was just a baby, so I can't say I remember, but from what I've been told, those first few years of assembling the dome were heroic. Now we live in comfort. I've got a computer that lets me download e-entertainment from Earth by satellite, and the gardens that were planted when I was a kid make parts of the dome seem like a tropical garden. It isn't a bad place to live.

But now it could become a bad place to die. . . .

Let me say this to anyone on Earth who might

read this. If, like me, you have legs that don't work, Mars, with its lower gravity pull, is probably a better place to be than Earth.

That's only a guess, of course, because I haven't had the chance to compare Mars' gravity to Earth's gravity. In fact, I'm the only person in the entire history of mankind who has never been on Earth.

I'm not kidding.

You see, I'm the first person born on Mars. Everyone else here came from Earth nearly eight Martian years ago—15 Earth years to you—as part of the first expedition to set up a colony. The trip took eight months, and during this voyage my mother and father fell in love.

I smiled. I'd forgotten about that. Back when Mom and Dad first came to Mars, the trip from Mars to Earth had taken eight months. And in just 18 years, scientists had been able to take two months off that time. We were really speeding through space now!

I went back to my first journal entry.

Mom is a leading plant biologist. Dad is a space pilot. They were the first couple to be married on Mars. And the last, for now. They loved each other so much that they married by exchanging their vows over radio phone with a preacher on Earth. When I was born half a Mars year later—which now makes me 14 Earth years old—it made things so complicated on the colony that it was decided there would be no more marriages and babies until the colony was better established.

What was complicated about a baby on Mars?

Let me put it this way. Because of planetary orbits, spaceships can reach Mars only every three years. (Only four ships have arrived since I was born.) And for what it costs to send a ship from Earth, cargo space is expensive. Very, very expensive. Diapers, baby bottles, cribs, and carriages are not exactly a priority for interplanetary travel.

I did without all that stuff. In fact, my wheelchair isn't even motorized, because every extra pound of cargo costs something like 10,000 dollars.

Just like I did without a modern hospital when I was born. So when my spinal column twisted funny during birth and damaged the nerves to my legs, there was no one to fix them. Which is why I'm in a wheelchair.

But it could be worse. On Earth, I'd weigh 110 pounds. Here, I'm only 42 pounds, so I don't have to fight gravity nearly as hard as Earth kids.

I had written that when I had barely turned 14 in Earth years. I knew now, of course, that the spinal damage hadn't been an accident. But a lot of things had happened since that first journal entry. On Mars, Terratakers had tried taking over the dome. They'd tried to fake evidence of an ancient civilization and then attempted to gain control of a space torpedo that would let them dominate the Earth. And on Earth, they'd tried to kill all the vice governors of the World United Federation. They'd forced us robot-control kids to become an army of soldier robots.

And in the middle of all that had been my only journey away from Mars.

I saw the entry I'd written during the space trip to Earth nearly three years earlier, and I remembered the incredible feeling of homesickness.

A little over two weeks ago, I was on Mars. Under the dome. Living life in a wheelchair. . . . Then, with the suddenness of a lightning bolt, I discovered I would be returning to Earth with Dad as he piloted this spaceship on the three-year round-trip to Earth and back to Mars. . . .

I'd been dreaming of Earth for years.

After all, I was the only human in the history of mankind who had never been on the planet. I'd only been able to watch it through the telescope and wonder about snowcapped mountains and blue sky and rain and oceans and rivers and trees and flowers and birds and animals.

Earth.

When Rawling had told me I was going to visit Earth, I'd been too excited to sleep. Finally, I'd be able to see everything I'd only read about under the cramped protection of the Mars Dome, where it never rained, the sky outside was the color of butterscotch, and the mountains were dusty red.

But when it came time to roll onto the shuttle that would take us to the *Moon Racer*, waiting in orbit around Mars, I had discovered an entirely new sensation. Homesickness. Mars—and the dome—was all I knew.

Dozens of technicians and scientists had been there when we left, surprising me by their cheers and affection. Rawling had been the second-to-last person to say good-bye, shaking my hand gravely, then giving me a hug.

And the last person?

That had been Mom, biting her lower lip and blinking back tears. It hurt so much seeing her sad— and feeling my own sadness. I'd nearly rolled my wheelchair away from the shuttle. At that moment three years seemed like an eternity. I knew that if an accident happened anywhere along the 100 million miles of travel to Earth and back, I might never see her again. Mom must have been able to read my thoughts because she'd leaned forward to kiss me and told me to not even dare think about staying. She'd whispered that although she'd miss me, she knew I was in God's hands, so I wouldn't be alone. She said she was proud of me for taking this big step, and she'd pray every day for the safe return of me and Dad.

The first few nights on the spaceship had not been easy. Alone in my bunk I had stared upward in the darkness for hours and hours, surprised at how much the sensation of homesickness could fill my stomach.

Who would think that a person could miss a place that would kill you if you walked outside without a space suit. . . .

Since that journey to Earth, these three years had passed. I was 17 now. I'd seen robot-control technology get better and better. In fact, in comparison to some of the kids just learning, I was considered an old pioneer of robot control. Just like Ashley.

Yet, exciting as Earth was, I always missed Mars.

Our fleet was so close now—that after three years—within 24 hours I would finally be back.

Home.

Where now it looked like immediately I'd have to help start a defense against the first attempted planetary invasion in the history of humankind.

CHAPTER 8

We didn't land on Mars.

Instead, Dad hooked up our spaceship to the Habitat Lander, a shuttle permanently parked in orbit around Mars. The shuttle was designed to take passengers and equipment down to Mars from the larger spaceships that arrived from Earth.

While it was routine, it was still tricky. If Dad came into the friction of Mars' atmosphere too steeply, the heat would overcome the disposable heat shield and burn the shuttle to cinders. Too shallow, and the Habitat Lander would bounce off the atmosphere toward Jupiter.

Because of my body cast, I was the last one to get strapped in. But at least we were still in low gravity. I wasn't looking forward to being on the surface, where people would have to move me around like a piece of furniture.

By now Dad, Ashley, all the other kids in the shuttle, and I knew each other very well. Traveling through space for months in a vehicle with as much living space as a house would do that.

"Ready, guys?" Dad asked.

There were a few cheers and nods. I looked at the faces around me. All these kids had become my friends over the past several years since Ashley and I had helped rescue them. Some, like Joey, seemed nervous. Others, like Michael and Ingrid, looked excited. I reminded myself that except for Ashley and Dad, none of them had been on the red planet before.

Dad hit a few buttons. The hatchway between the shuttle and our spaceship sealed. The Habitat Lander's rockets fired softly, and the shuttle moved away from the spaceship. The spaceship would stay in orbit until the return trip to Earth.

Five minutes later, Dad aimed the nose of the Habitat Lander at the top of Mars' atmosphere.

I knew that a lot of people from the dome would be outside in a platform buggy watching the night sky anxiously for the brightness of our approaching shuttle. The supplies that came with our fleet were crucial to their survival.

If the Habitat Lander crashed, our deaths would be quick and theirs a lot slower.

I prayed, taking comfort in knowing that because of God's love for us, death isn't the worst thing that can happen to a person.

And then the bumping began as we hit the top of the atmosphere.

Dad had warned us to expect a roller-coaster ride, and he was right.

First came the tumbling around as the atmosphere thickened. Loud screaming filled the air inside the shuttle. But it wasn't any of us. It was the shrieking of the heat shield against the intense friction of Mars' atmosphere.

Next came a *clunk* and the dropping of the heat shield.

Then the *pop* of opening parachutes. It felt like a giant hand had just jerked us upward. That's when I got my first reminder of gravity after six months of weightlessness.

The roar of the retro-rockets guided our landing.

And finally, a soft *bump* as we landed.

The shuttle exploded with cheers.

I was home.

"Tyce?"

"Mom!"

Boy, did she look good. Her thick, dark hair was still cut short, like an upside-down bowl, but this time she'd carefully styled it. For the first time I saw a streak of gray.

Lying on my back on the floor of the platform buggy, I grinned at her, despite how dumb I felt.

Although she was smiling, her eyes were searching me.

It had taken at least a half hour for Ashley and Dad to get me in a space suit so I could be transported from the shuttle to the platform buggy. Once inside the safety of the mini-dome of the platform buggy, I'd removed my space helmet.

"Tyce!" Mom exclaimed again. Seeing me in a body cast was no surprise to her, I could tell. We'd been able to send e-mails back and forth the whole time I was in space. She leaned down quickly, then hesitated.

I guessed what she was thinking. That maybe after three years I was too grown-up to be affectionate. Especially in front of the other kids in the platform buggy.

"Mom! Don't I get a hug?" I said enthusiastically.

Her lips curved in a big grin and she hugged me as best as she could. Even though I was in a body cast wrapped in a space suit, that hug felt great.

When she let go of me, there was a single, shiny trail of a tear on her cheek. "I'm glad you're home," she said.

"Me too."

Mom stood and hugged Dad, then kept holding on to his hand. This time seeing their embrace didn't bug me, as it had earlier times when Dad had come home to Mars. It was good to see them together again.

My homecoming on Mars would have been perfect. I saw

Flip and Flop, the two Martian koalas I'd rescued from death. It was great being in my own bed. The other kids had settled into their temporary quarters. And it felt very right being with both Mom and Dad again.

Yes, my homecoming would have been totally perfect.

Except for an emergency air leak the next morning that threatened to kill everyone under the dome.

CHAPTER 9

Just after breakfast, I was in a wheelchair in Rawling's office. It had been great to see his smiling face as soon as I was carried into the dome.

Already I missed zero gravity. The seat back of the wheelchair had been tilted so my body could recline. Before, when I was in a regular wheelchair without a body cast, at least I could wheel myself around the dome. Now, lying close to horizontal with the cast holding my body rigid, I was totally dependent on other people to move me.

Which was why I was in Rawling's office, where the walls still displayed framed paintings of Earth scenes like sunsets and mountains. I knew Rawling hated the paintings because of what they stood for—that the previous director,

Blaine Steven, had used valuable and expensive cargo space to bring such things to Mars for his office. And because of his role in almost killing 180 people under the dome during the oxygen crisis, Steven was still in a World United Federation prison on Earth. But he didn't seem to mind. At least he was safe from the Terrataker rebels who had threatened to kill him.

So why were the paintings still there? I grinned. It was typical of Rawling to take his responsibilities so seriously that he didn't even take the time to remove the paintings. After all, he was the current director of the Mars Project and also one of only two medical doctors under the dome.

"How long?" I asked—for the 12th time in the last few minutes. Rawling had just passed an X-ray wand over me. On the floor was the lead shield that he'd wrapped around the parts of my body that weren't being X-rayed.

"Just waiting for the film to print out. I'll compare it to the doctor's notes that were e-mailed from Earth. Then, finally, I'll be able to give you an answer. I refuse to guess until then."

For me, Rawling was a mixture of older brother—in his late 40s, much older!—buddy, teacher, and doctor. Rawling had worked with me for hours every day ever since I was eight years old, training me in a virtual-reality program to control a robot body as if it were my own. His short, dark hair was even more streaked with gray than I remembered. His nose still looked like it had been broken once, which it had. When he was younger he'd been a quarterback at his university back on Earth, and his wide shoulders showed it.

"I think it's finished printing," I said rather impatiently.

"Old age has made you cranky, huh?" he replied wryly.

He still had the same dry sense of humor I remembered. Although 17 was a lot older than when I'd last seen him, it didn't seem like three years had passed. It felt so good to be around him again.

"No, this body cast." I was already feeling itchy, and it wasn't even close to time for the body powder.

Rawling leisurely got out of his chair, grinning because he knew I was impatient. He read the X-ray film, then looked up at me.

"Well?" I said.

"Well, what?" he threw back.

"Lost your eyesight since I was last here?" I knew him well enough to tease him. "Need bifocals?"

"Ouch, not even funny," he said. "Because it's true." He laughed, then scanned the medical charts from Earth again. "Your dad must be exhausted. How many shuttle trips are he and the other pilots making?"

"Quit stalling." I knew Rawling already knew. Each shuttle trip took two hours. Dad had to make one shuttle trip for each spaceship but could do only five trips per day. Ours was the only one that had been unloaded last night, since it was so late in the evening. Today some of the passenger spaceships would be unloaded. For the passengers in the other spaceships, one extra day in space wouldn't seem too long, not after the length of the trip. After that, Dad would bring down the equipment and supplies from the unmanned ships. And then the major work would begin. Assembling the carbon-dioxide generators. In the meantime, the other kids were getting a tour of the dome and settling into their new home.

"Stalling?" Rawling asked as innocently as possible. "You accuse *me* of stalling?"

"When can I get the body cast off?"

He smiled and read the X-rays one more time. I tried to grab them from him, but he was just out of reach. My arms flailed.

"You can feel your leg and wiggle your toes, right? That's good news."

I groaned. "Come on, Rawling. I already showed you. It's no fun in this body cast. When can we get rid of it?"

Suddenly serious, he scratched his chin. "The X-rays show something strange here. At the bottom of your spine. If I didn't know better, I'd say it was an implanted pacemaker. Except smaller."

"I know what it is. It sends out small electrical impulses that are supposed to help the nerves splice better."

"I don't see mention of it on the charts."

"Well," I said, "that's what one of the doctors told me. All I care about anyway is getting this cast off. When!"

He grinned again. "Tomorrow."

"All right!" I said.

And that's when the dome horns began to scream.

We both knew what it meant. The horns blew for only one reason.

"Oxygen alert!" he shouted above the horns. "Got to go!"

He did.

Seconds later he reappeared with a mask and oxygen tube. He strapped the mask over my face. "If you can't breathe, all you need to do is twist the top of the tube to release the oxygen!"

All across the dome everyone else was doing the same thing. It had been drilled into us again and again. It was the first thing new arrivals learned. When the horns signal an oxygen emergency, go for an oxygen tube. There were at least two in every living area. And dozens and dozens of others scattered across the dome. It meant that anybody at anytime could reach one within 10 seconds of hearing the sirens. Each tube had enough oxygen to last 30 minutes.

"Get one for you too!" I yelled at Rawling. Not that he was likely to forget.

He nodded. "Got to go!"

With that, he was gone.

CHAPTER 10

Ashley rescued me.

Not that I was dying, but it was very frustrating to be stuck in Rawling's office in a body cast in a wheelchair with loud horns vibrating your head and an oxygen mask on your face.

She ran in, her black hair flying around the edges of her own mask. "Rawling said you'd be here!" The only way to communicate was by shouting from beneath the mask. "You all right?"

I nodded. "What's happening?"

"Something punctured the dome!"

"Big hole?"

"The size of a baseball. You should have seen the stuff getting sucked through the hole!"

I could imagine it. The dome was made of a thick, black glass and was powered by huge solar panels hung right below the roof. The dome was pressurized, of course, so air would have escaped through that hole with hurricane force.

"Can you take me out there?" I yelled.

"What?" Ashley exclaimed above the horns.

"Can you—?" I stopped shouting. The horns had finally quit. Someone must have been able to put an emergency patch over the hole. Suction from the outer atmosphere would keep it in place while it was permanently repaired.

I smiled weakly as we both removed our masks. "Can you take me out there?"

"Sure," she said. "But how about you leave this body of yours behind for now."

I knew exactly what she meant. I looked at my watch. "Good idea. We've got time."

"Time before what?"

I didn't answer. My next headache was scheduled to arrive in exactly an hour.

"I'll explain when I can," I promised. "Trust me, all right?"

After wheeling me to the computer room, Ashley hooked me to the X-ray transmitter that would put me in contact with my robot, which had already been unloaded and was parked at the far end of the dome.

Ashley ran me through the checklist.

"Check, check, and check," I said. "I'm ready for the helmet."

She lowered it on my head, then snapped the visor in place.

My world instantly became black. The only sound was the faint *whoosh, whoosh* of my heartbeat.

In the darkness I gave a thumbs-up, knowing Ashley was waiting for the signal that I was ready.

I waited too. For a familiar sensation, as if I were falling, falling, falling off an invisible cliff into total blackness.

The sensation came.

And I fell, fell, fell. . . .

CHAPTER 11

At the entrance to the dome, light entered the video lenses of my robot where it was parked. Through the robot, I saw movement everywhere just inside the entrance of the dome. The emergency patch had stopped most of the immediate air loss, but repair crews now had to go outside. Nearby, 10 men and women geared up in space suits carried various pieces of equipment as the inner door of the entrance slid open.

If you can picture an igloo large enough to fit 10 people, with that short, rounded tunnel sticking out in front, you'll have a good idea of what the entrance to the dome looks like.

In our case, there are two large sealed doors to the tunnel. The outer door leads to the surface of the planet. The inner door leads to the inside of the dome. Between those doors is a gap about twice the length of a platform buggy, where one of them was parked.

As I watched, all 10 crew members climbed the ladder and entered the minidome of the platform buggy. The inner door closed and sealed the dome again.

The outer door opened. Instantly the warm, moist, oxygen-filled air from the tunnel turned into white, ghostly vapor and escaped into the cold Martian atmosphere. There was no danger to the rest of the dome, of course, because the inner door was still sealed to keep the dome's air from escaping.

The platform buggy rolled out onto the surface of the planet.

As the outer door began to shut again, another crew member, who had already been outside, stepped into the tunnel chamber. He moved slowly because his bulky space suit made him clumsy. When the outer door sealed shut, he hit a button to open the inner door. A brief puff of vapor showed where Martian air was absorbed into the dome air.

I guessed this crew member had been the first one out there to survey the situation.

I was curious to know what could have penetrated the dome and caused the leak. So I commanded the robot to roll forward.

The man kept walking away, so I sped up to get his

attention. It didn't take much extra speed. His space suit slowed him down considerably.

He didn't see me so I tapped him on the shoulder with the titanium robot fingers. The crew member tilted his face toward me. I didn't see it. Space-suit helmets have extremely dark visors.

"Hello," I said. "I am Tyce Sanders. What happened out there?"

The man stopped walking immediately. Now that I had his attention, I waited for him to pull off his helmet. After all, he was in the dome now. He didn't have to worry about the Martian atmosphere.

Instead, he did something strange. Still wearing his space suit, he wriggled his right arm free. The empty sleeve of his space suit hung at his side, but his right arm remained against his body inside the space suit, as if he were searching desperately for something.

"Hello," I repeated more slowly, just in case he hadn't understood me the first time. "What happened out there?"

I never got an answer.

The man looked at me and then pressed something inside his suit.

Instantly it seemed like a baseball bat had slammed against the side of my head. Not the robot's head. But my head. Where I was lying in my body cast in the computer room.

I screamed at the incredible pain but didn't hear anything because my helmet blocked all sound.

I screamed and screamed until, mercifully, the pain inside my brain must have knocked me totally unconscious.

CHAPTER 12

"Here's what's strange about the hole in the dome," Dad said the next morning.

The pain from my headache had been so intense that I hadn't even woken up until afternoon the day before. And then I'd had to just lie there and rest, until Mom and Dad came to get me.

Now the three of us—Mom, Dad, and I—were sitting in the small eating area of our minidome. Our minidome, like everyone else's, had two office-bedrooms with a common living space in the middle. But Mom and Dad weren't able to use their second room as an office because it had become my bedroom. We didn't need a kitchen, because we never had anything to cook. Instead, a microwave oven hung on the far wall. It was used to heat nutrient tubes, or nute tubes, as we called them for short. Another door at the back of the living space led to a small bathroom. It wasn't much. Compared to Earth homes, our minidome had less space in it than two average bedrooms.

"Head height," Mom said, sipping on real Earth coffee. I'd brought some back for her, knowing how much she liked it. "No asteroid would come in at that level. I also heard the clean-up crew didn't find anything inside to show what had hit the dome with such impact. So what could have caused it?"

Dad grinned. "It's obvious Tyce got his brains from you."

She kissed his cheek. "And his good looks from you."

"Please," I said, from the horizontal discomfort of my wheelchair. "I feel lousy enough in this body cast. Then to have you two mooning over each other like high school sweethearts . . ."

They both laughed. They knew I didn't mind that much.

Dad took a slurp of his coffee. "Rawling tells me the hole was a perfect circle."

"Not an accident?" I said.

Dad shook his head. "An explosive device is Rawling's best guess."

"But who would do it?"

"That's another weird thing. The dome's mainframe automatically keeps a time log. It doesn't appear that anyone left the dome. It's like someone had been camping out there, waiting to somehow punch the hole." Dad paused. "That's why Rawling would like to send you and Ashley out there to look around."

He grinned at the frown on my face. "Don't worry. Rawling can wait until after your body cast is removed."

"You're not going to like what you see, Tyce," Rawling said gently, a couple of hours after breakfast. "Over eight months your muscles will have wasted away."

I lay facedown on a cot in the small, sterile, square medical room. A zipper down the back and one on each side held the body cast together.

"Didn't have much on my legs to begin with," I answered. "And I'll close my eyes if I don't like the rest of what I see." Although my words were brave, my stomach had the willies.

"I'm also saying that without healthy muscles, you can't expect to roll off this bed and walk out the door. It's going to take some work before you find out if the operation was completely successful."

Different doctors had already warned me a dozen times that it would take a lot of painful physical therapy and endless hours of exercise. That didn't matter. If I could walk, I'd gladly pay that price a million times over.

"I'm ready, Rawling. Please, please, please, just unzip this stupid thing. I want out."

I heard him unzip the left side of the body cast. He spoke casually. "Ashley says she found you in the computer lab yesterday. Screaming. And then you passed out, and she couldn't wake you up for several hours. Plus, your robot was abandoned at the entrance to the dome. Care to tell me about it?"

I took a deep breath. "It was a bad headache that disconnected me. Don't tell Mom or Dad. I don't want them worried. I'm sure the headaches will go away."

Another zip. *"Headaches?* You've had more than one? Tell me as your doctor, not as a friend you don't want to worry."

I told him. All of it.

He unzipped the final panel of the body cast. "Have you had trouble with your vision?"

"No," I said. "Just headaches."

"At least that probably eliminates a tumor or something really bad. Let's look into it once we get this done." He lifted off the back and both sides of the body cast. Cool air hit my skin. I felt him place something over the middle of my body.

"What was that?" I asked.

"A towel. It's very encouraging that you felt it. It confirms that the splicing of your spinal nerves was successful."

I wanted to sing with joy—or, even better, dance. But I figured that would take a while. If it was possible . . .

"Keep the towel in place while I roll you over and off the front piece of the body cast," Rawling said. "Then I'll help you sit."

I was about to answer when someone knocked loudly on the door.

"Hang on," Rawling called. "Two minutes."

"It's me," a voice said. My dad's voice.

"Want him in?" Rawling asked.

"Sure. As soon as you have me sitting."

That took another minute.

And that's how Dad found me. On a chair. Sitting. Wrapped in a towel around my midsection. With a blanket around me to keep me warm.

"Toothpick, huh," I said to them both. I opened my blanket and looked down at my body. After eight months in a cast, I was just skin and bones.

"Wiggle your toes," Rawling said.

I was scared. What if only my toes worked? I wiggled them. They moved. But I wasn't surprised at that. They'd moved when I was in the body cast. Without waiting for instruction from Rawling, I tried to swing my legs at the knees.

I felt stabs of pain. Water filled my eyes. But not from the pain. "Did you see that?" I almost yelled.

"It wasn't a breeze, was it?" Rawling answered. "Your feet actually swung a little."

"Yes," I said. I did it again. They moved only a fraction of an inch, but they moved. *My legs work!*

Rawling cleared his throat a couple of times and looked at my dad.

I saw my dad swallow hard, as if he were trying to say something. Then I realized he, too, was fighting tears.

"I think," Rawling said, his voice shaky, "that the operation was successful. But that doesn't mean you can walk. Yet. Build up the muscles with exercise and go slow. Then you can learn to walk."

You can walk. What a sweet, sweet phrase. After a lifetime in a wheelchair, I could hardly believe it. I turned to Dad with a big smile.

Dad's face, however, was troubled.

"Dad?" I said quietly, not understanding his reaction to the news that I could walk. Really walk! Didn't he want me to be able to walk? Or was something else bothering him?

"Tyce, I'm so . . . happy for you . . . for all of us. What great news!" he exclaimed finally. "I wish I could wait and let us all celebrate a while longer," he said slowly and sadly. "But I just found out that we've lost all communication with Earth. The techie guys came and told me since they couldn't find you."

"All communication? Impossible." This came from Rawling.

"They said the dome's mainframe computer is malfunctioning," Dad answered.

"The hard drive can't be down," Rawling argued. "The rest of the dome is running fine. And we've got two backup mainframes."

"Rawling," Dad answered patiently, "all I know is what the computer techies told me. Some virus has wiped out all the software in the communications segment of the hard drive. We can't reach Earth. Earth can't reach us."

"We've got backup software. They can reinstall it," Rawling insisted.

Dad shook his head. "It has disappeared. And with no link to Earth, there's no way to download another copy."

The room went silent as we thought about what that meant.

Rawling closed his eyes. "No communication with Earth. The Manchurian fleet approaches. How much worse can this get?"

Dad coughed.

Rawling opened his eyes and stared at him. "You're telling me this *can* get worse?"

"The surface-to-space missile system that arrived with us. We haven't had time to put it in place, of course. But I don't know if it will do any good. All the trigger devices are gone."

"Gone? Impossible. We've had that equipment securely locked down. And under video surveillance."

"That's just it, Rawling. While you've been in here with Tyce, I asked to review the video surveillance from the minute the equipment was being unloaded up until now. No one has been near it here on Mars. It looks like the trigger devices were missing before I even brought the stuff down on the shuttle. But how could that be? Our last message from Earth confirmed that the trigger devices had been sent with the equipment."

"So you're telling me the impossible." Rawling rubbed his face. "Someone stole them in the six months of travel between Earth and Mars. In outer space. On an unmanned ship."

Dad nodded. "That's about it. And now we've got a hostile Manchurian space fleet approaching, no communication with Earth, and no weapons to protect us." He gave me a weak smile. "But at least Tyce should be able to walk soon."

I'm not sure it was much of a consolation if Mars was going to be invaded.

CHAPTER 13

Butterscotch sky. Blue sun edging over the outline of distant mountains. It was still morning, so wisps of blue cloud still appeared in the sky. They'd disappear when the day became warmer.

There was no oxygen, and a wind of 80 miles an hour rattled sand against the titanium of our robots. It was minus 100 degrees Fahrenheit.

That's what it was like outside the Mars Dome as I rolled my robot body across the packed red soil with Ashley's robot beside it.

It was around 11 o'clock. Only an hour had passed since Dad had shared his grim news.

Inside the dome, Ashley and I were hooked to the computers. As were all the other kids who controlled robots. They had sent their robots to the first carbon-dioxide generator site, a half mile away from the dome, to unpack the crates that held the equipment. This had been the first equipment unloaded by shuttle from the unmanned spaceships above us in orbit.

The harsh Martian environment was the reason for the robots. Robots could work outside more easily and faster than humans in space suits. There was far less danger too. A hole in a space suit could mean death for a human. In fact, without the strength of the titanium robots and their ability to work outside, it would have been nearly impossible to assemble the generators. Engineers calculated it would have otherwise taken thousands of human workers, and the dome couldn't sustain all those people.

"I hope we find something that will help Rawling," Ashley's robot said to mine. We were hooked up by wireless audio. "Everyone is pretty nervous about the Manchurian space fleet."

"Maybe not everyone," I answered. Ashley and I were directing our robots to the repaired puncture of the dome. "Perhaps someone is helping them from this end."

That was the reason for the communications breakdown. As we had found out this afternoon, someone under the dome had introduced the virus to wipe out the communications software on the mainframe. And that same person had stolen the backup disks. The same person who had found a way to get outside the dome and somehow put a small hole in it? But who? There were 200 scientists and techies, plus another 50 robot-control kids.

We rolled our robots around the outer edge of the dome.

"Here it is," I said, pointing at the patch.

The dome towered high above our robots, gleaming black in the weak sunlight.

"Another thing I don't get," Ashley said, "is why. If Rawling is right and someone somehow got out of the dome to do this, what would it gain him or her? I mean, the emergency patch was in place in less than five minutes. And why try to harm the dome if you have to live in it too?"

I didn't have an answer, so I couldn't give her one. Instead I searched the ground with the visual signals sent to my brain through the robot's video lenses.

All I saw were footsteps. Dozens and dozens. Which made sense. This was where the repair crew had spent hours putting the permanent patch in place. If one person had once stood here and done something at head height to cause the hole, his or her footprints were long destroyed.

"Where are you going?" Ashley asked as I directed my robot to begin rolling away from the dome.

"Just wondering if I can see anything better from a distance," I answered. "I—"

"You what?"

"Come here!"

Ashley's robot rolled to meet mine. We were less than 20 human steps away from the wall of the dome.

"Look at these tracks," I said.

"Tire tracks. It's where the platform buggy stopped. And here's where everyone climbed down."

"Yes. But what about those footprints there?" My robot arm pointed away from the dome at a single set of footprints. "See? The footprints end at the edge of the platform buggy tire tracks. That means the footprints were there first. And the tire tracks ran them over after. And there's something else."

"The footprints are walking *toward* the dome."

"Exactly," I told Ashley. "And it's the only set of footprints. So where did this person come from?"

"That should be easy to answer. We just track the footprints backward."

We found the answer two miles away. Over a hill. Hidden from the dome.

When we found the answer, we didn't bother wasting any time. We disconnected immediately, leaving the robots near what we had found.

Back in the computer lab, we took off our helmets and helped each other disconnect.

Ashley helped me into my wheelchair since my legs were still so weak. Usually I insisted on pushing myself. Not this time.

She raced my wheelchair forward, from the computer lab toward Rawling's office.

We had to talk to him as soon as possible.

CHAPTER 14

Forty-five minutes later, Mom, Dad, and Rawling stood behind my wheelchair in Rawling's office. Ashley sat beside me. The lights were dim, and a large TV screen was flickering.

"Ready?" Rawling asked.

He must have taken our silence as a yes since he hit a button on his remote. The screen darkened briefly. Then it showed the eerie reds and oranges of the Martian landscape.

I knew what we would see. This visual input had just been recorded through my robot's computer. Because the robot was on wheels, it was a steady image. It showed the footprints that Ashley and I had followed. It showed the hill we had first climbed and then descended. And, on the other side, hidden beneath an outcropping, it showed what we had found.

A small shuttle ship.

Dad whistled. "That's a two-person ship. Mainly used on the Moon to take people up to orbiting spaceships."

Next the visual lurched a little. My robot had rolled into a small depression as I brought it in for a closer look. Then the visual zoomed in close on a symbol on the side of the shuttle.

"Manchurian!" Mom exclaimed. "That's the shape of a Manchurian flag."

The image on the television suddenly went dark. That was the point where Ashley and I had decided to disengage from our robots and find Rawling immediately.

Rawling moved to the wall of his office and hit the light switch. "As you know," he said, pacing the floor, "Ashley and Tyce found this with their robots an hour ago. Unless we are reading this totally wrong, it looks like someone landed in the shuttle—"

"But from where?" Dad interrupted. "Something that small can't travel more than 1,000 miles. It doesn't hold the oxygen and food needed to travel here from Earth or the Moon."

"I can't guess where at this point," Rawling answered. "For now, let's just stick with what we know from the evidence."

"The footprints led away from the abandoned shuttle toward the dome," Mom said.

"More specifically, toward the point of puncture of the dome," Rawling added. "We can guess that the person used some device, maybe an explosive, to punch the hole through about head height. But why? And then what?"

I had a mental image of a man with a space suit walking into the tunnel of the dome. And then the answer hit me. "To create a diversion. Earlier we couldn't figure out why someone would make a puncture that was so easy to repair. Because it only made for temporary confusion. And it also guaranteed that the main entrance to the dome would be opened for that person as the repair crews went out."

I told them about the person in the space suit. "That must have been the space-shuttle pilot. All he or she had to do was get inside, never to be noticed with all the new people and new activity. There are plenty of places to hide if no one is looking for you."

"And I'll bet once he got inside," Rawling said, speaking slowly as he thought aloud, "the next thing he did was disable the communications system."

Mom gripped my shoulder. "I don't suppose you had your robot's visual on record when you approached this person."

"No," I said. "I was just trying to get some freedom. Then the—" I was almost about to say "headache hit me." But so far I'd only told Rawling. This definitely wasn't the time to burden Mom and Dad with something so minor, compared to the crisis of the dome.

"Then the . . . ?" Mom prompted.

Then came a horrible thought. "Dad, remember in space

when you told me the Manchurians would never destroy the dome itself?"

He nodded. "I said the fleet would never fire any weapons on the dome. That they would want to be able to land and send in soldiers because it was important they get Mars with the dome and the generators intact."

"And you said you couldn't figure out why the fleet would follow us, knowing we have the surface-to-space atomic weapons to protect us."

"The triggers!" Ashley said. "Stolen. Now the missiles won't work. Do you think . . . ?"

Suddenly all the pieces of the puzzle snapped together in my brain. "I think I can guess why the fleet is on its way. They've sent someone ahead. One person. And he was to be inside the dome. Preparing it for the arrival of the fleet."

CHAPTER 15

"Ugly," Ashley said at 3:30 that afternoon.

"Hey," I protested. She had just arrived at my minidome, where I had been waiting for her after eating a quick lunch. "This is me you're talking about."

In my lap were a blanket, a pair of binoculars, and a stuffed pillowcase. Sewn onto the pillowcase were two arms made of tubes of cloth filled with rags. Mom had helped me sew a crude head, made of a smaller stuffed pillowcase, on top.

I held it up for more inspection. "For half a body, it might just work as a decoy. Think the guy in the space suit will believe it's me?"

"Let's hope so. You ready?"

I jammed the half-body back on top of the binoculars in my lap. I covered it with a blanket. "Ready. Take me to the top."

Ashley wheeled me to the observatory on the third-level deck of the dome. It was a short trip. After all, the total area of the dome was only about four of Earth's football fields. The main level of the dome held the minidomes and labs. One level up, a walkway about 10 feet wide circled the inside of the dome walls. The third level, centered at the top of the dome, could be reached only by a narrow catwalk from the second level.

The floor of it was a circle only 15 feet wide. It hung directly below the ceiling, above the exact middle of the main level. Here a powerful telescope perched beneath a round bubble of clear, thick glass that stuck up from the black glass that made up the rest of the dome. From there, the massive telescope gave an incredible view of the solar system.

It was my favorite place in the dome. I'd spent a lot of hours there—observing the stars, asteroids, and planets. And also asking "why" questions about God and the universe. Every time I was up here, I marveled again at how God had created everything—all the "matter"—and then made it work together, in some kind of perfect harmony that scientists could find no natural explanation for. It had been through all my hours spent in the observatory, as well as all the crises I'd faced on Mars before going to Earth, that I'd come to believe that I had a soul—a part of me invisible to science and medicine. A part of me that feels love, happiness, hope, and sadness. A part of me that knows God loves us and yet still wonders why God can allow bad things to happen to us . . . like the pending Manchurian invasion.

I shook off the deep thoughts.

Ashley parked the wheelchair in front of the telescope eyepieces. I set the brakes and lifted the blanket off me. I gave Ashley the binoculars, which she set on the floor.

"This is the tricky part," I said, lifting the half-body out of my lap. "Can you prop this behind my back?"

I leaned forward. She quickly shoved the stuffed pillow-cases between my back and the wheelchair, making sure the fake head was right behind my own head.

"Now the arms," I said.

As we had planned beforehand, Ashley lifted the half-body's arms to the telescope controls. She taped them in place, its arms wrapped around my face, to make sure we had the height and angle right—so the dummy would look like a real person. We wanted it at the telescope so I could look down on the dome from a more hidden position.

With the dummy in position, Ashley held my arms and helped lower me beneath the dummy's arms as I wiggled feet forward out of the wheelchair. It was strange to actually feel the floor of the observatory against my legs. Even though my muscles were weak, I was able to roll over onto my belly. I glanced upward at the wheelchair.

Ashley was already moving the dummy's head forward

against the eyepieces. She taped it in place too. "What do you think?"

"People hardly ever think to look up here anytime," I said, "so we're probably safe 'til nightfall." Right now it was 3:30 in the afternoon. The weak sunlight was already fading. It couldn't penetrate the black superglass of the dome. "And if anyone does look up here, it's dim enough that I think the outline will fool anyone into thinking I'm still in my wheelchair. Just to be sure, take a look once you get down, and call me on the wrist buzzer."

Ashley knelt beside me. She had carried two wrist buzzers—small communicating devices that looked just like watches. She gave me one and kept the other.

"See you in a while," she said. "I'll come back later as planned to help you back into your wheelchair. In the meantime, if you need anything, just buzz me."

"Thanks."

As she left, I crawled to the edge of the observatory floor with my binoculars beside me.

Two minutes later the wrist buzzer crackled.

"Fooled me," Ashley said. "And I knew what to look for."

"Good," I answered.

Now I was ready to watch as long as it took to spot the intruder. Even better, I'd have a surprise waiting!

CHAPTER 16

I surveyed the area below.

I could see the minidomes and the experimental labs and open areas, where equipment was maintained. Some people were using the second-level walkway for exercise, jogging in circles above the main floor below.

The dome now held the original 200 people, plus the other 50 who had arrived with the space fleet. In terms of living space, it was a lot more crowded. But as soon as the carbon-dioxide generators were built, expansion of the dome would be next. In the meantime, three research areas had been temporarily shut down.

In the first research area, a minidome had been erected as a huge dorm area for all 50 robot-control kids.

And the last two research areas had been converted to a

computer area, holding cots and transmitters for all the kids when they were using their robot-control capabilities to work on the generators. According to strict instructions from the World United Federation, the kids were only allowed to control the robots in shifts of four hours a day. Then they were free to follow up on schoolwork and have playtime.

Right now, many of the kids were hooked up. As they lay on cots, each wore a helmet to block out the sights and sounds of the dome. Each was busy controlling a robot that was working at the carbon-dioxide generator site.

This time it wasn't any of the kids I was worried about. No, I was watching for an adult who was doing something unusual.

More specifically—although I hadn't told anyone because it seemed too dumb—I was watching for the one person I knew who had enough computer skills to hack his way into the mainframe computer. It was something he had done before. And even though I couldn't believe he had somehow returned, my gut told me he had to be the one responsible.

I had learned the hard way. Of anyone in the Terrataker terrorist group that served the Manchurians, he was the genius who didn't care how many people died for him to get his way.

His name was Luke Daab. He'd masqueraded as a maintenance engineer—a sort of janitor—on the *Moon Racer.* After planning to crash the spaceship into the sun, he'd escaped in one of the pods. He'd last been reported hiding out in the Manchurian Sector of the Moon, a place that gave him diplomatic immunity from the World United Federation military. Now, impossible as it seemed, I wouldn't have been surprised if I saw him in my binoculars.

So as the minutes ticked by, I scanned the floor below. Stray thoughts hit me. My stomach began to growl.

Ashley had been right to accuse me earlier of filling my head with things because I was in a body cast and had little else to do.

Only now I was glad about it. Because—despite Rawling's quick check that didn't show a tumor—if there was seriously something in my brain that was causing these headaches, at least I knew that dying wouldn't be the worst thing to happen to me.

Some people say that science points us away from God, but I've learned that isn't true. The more and more I've learned about science—and the creation of the universe— the easier it is to believe that God is behind it.

On this space trip, I'd been reading a lot more about astronomy. And I was discovering that some astronomers believed that science clearly showed God had made this universe.

Like this weird detail, for instance. Physics shows that in the beginning moments of the universe, energy produced matter and antimatter. It might sound like comic-book stuff, but when particles of matter and particles of antimatter touch, both are destroyed. Physicists say that what should have happened is that all matter should have been exploded by antimatter. No matter should have survived anywhere. In fact, this universe should have become merely space with a weak radiation below the energy of a single microwave oven.

Instead—for no reason anyone in science can explain—for every 10 billion bits of antimatter, 10 billion and one bits of matter were created. The stuff left over—one bit for every 10 billion—was enough to make everything in the universe.

One mathematician figured out the chances that the universe would grow in such a way to support life. It was less than one in 10^{123}. That's a 10 followed by 123 zeros.

Somehow, against the odds of $1/10^{123}$, the universe grew in such a way to make life possible on Earth.

Is it so crazy for anyone to wonder if God was behind all of this?

It was now 5:30 in the afternoon. I had fought a headache for 10 minutes, grateful it wasn't so bad that I had to scream. That would have ruined my cover in a fairly small dome for sure.

When it passed, something strange caught my eye. A man was at the far wall of the dome. Away from the main traffic area. He was struggling to roll a huge cylindrical tank off a wagon.

It was dim there, and I could only see an outline of a figure.

Luke Daab! It had to be! The figure was skinny and short, just like him. And Luke had this weird hunched over way of walking, just like this guy.

But even more, I could see no reason for the tank to be placed there.

As I watched, the man took off with the wagon. A minute later he returned with another equally large tank. He looked around in all directions, as if making sure he was unseen. He rolled off the second tank, then hurried away.

Explosives? Getting them ready to detonate when the Manchurian fleet arrived? After all, if everyone in here were dead, the Manchurian soldiers wouldn't have to fight anyone.

I brought my wrist buzzer to my mouth as the small figure returned with a third container. "Ashley!" I hissed.

Seconds later, she replied, "Tyce!"

"Get Rawling," I said. I hadn't moved the binoculars from my eyes. The man was returning with a fourth tank. "Quick! Get Rawling or Dad and anyone else who can help on short notice and go to the south end of the dome. Grab the guy who's unloading some big cylinders. I haven't seen anything like them under the dome before. They could be explosives!"

CHAPTER 17

"Compressed oxygen," Rawling said an hour later.

I was back in my wheelchair, back in his office. It was 6:30—almost time for dinner. Ashley had helped me down from the upper deck, then gone to get something to eat.

Rawling waved some papers. "Here's the work order from the chief engineer. They're going to run some ventilation pipes around the inner wall of the dome. Then they're going to hook up those oxygen tanks to the pipes. Now that we've increased the dome's population, it's a backup system for the emergency oxygen tubes. If there's any threat to the dome's atmosphere, those big tanks of compressed oxygen will automatically release."

"Chief engineer's idea?"

"Straight from Earth." Rawling grimaced. "*Before* the

communications virus. All of the equipment was on one of the unmanned spaceships."

"What did he say about the guy unloading it?" I asked.

"He asked one of the techies to do it. I checked. You really think Luke is back?" he asked with raised eyebrows. Then he continued, "The techie *is* about the same size as Luke."

Rawling, too, knew what Luke Daab looked like. Daab had been a maintenance techie on Mars since the beginning of the Mars Project. Invisible as he worked, his job gave him access to absolutely everything under the dome.

"Someone came in on that two-person shuttle. It wouldn't surprise me if . . ." I stopped. "If that shuttle had been attached to one of the unmanned spaceships. It could happen, right? That near the Moon as the fleet is assembled, a Manchurian ship delivers Luke and the two-person shuttle to one of our unmanned ships. And they hitchhike across the solar system."

"The Manchurians do have the resources and technology to do that," Rawling said. Still, there was doubt in his voice. "But even if Luke got inside the unmanned ship—"

"That part would be easy. A hatch. He'd—"

"He'd still need oxygen and supplies for all those months of travel."

"Unloaded from the same Manchurian ship that brought him there."

"Maybe," Rawling said. "I'll send someone up in our own shuttle to take a close look at the unmanned vehicles in orbit.

In the meantime, I'm thinking of stopping all work, assembling everybody in one area of the dome, and doing a thorough search for whoever it is who sneaked in."

"It would be to our advantage," I argued, "if that person didn't know we knew about him. I can spend more time in the observatory looking for him, right? We've still got at least two months before the Manchurian fleet gets here."

"That dummy up there at the telescope does look pretty convincing from down below." Rawling grinned. "Much as we miss your help with the carbon-dioxide generators, maybe I can afford to give you a little more time. But try not to get too excited tonight when you see techies sealing off the temporary dome for the other kids."

"Sealing?"

"Part of that emergency backup plan. The World United Federation has literally invested billions in robot control. The future of Mars colonization depends on those 50 kids. So their sleeping area is being sealed. If anything happens to the pressure or oxygen level of the dome, at least they'll be safe until the problem is fixed."

"The adults can die first, huh," I said, making a bad joke.

"Let's face it," Rawling said. "Everything now depends on those who can control robots. Which includes you. So if you happen to see Luke Daab, don't go running after him. Got it?"

"That would be great, though," I said. "Being able to run. And finally stopping Luke Daab."

Rawling groaned. "I never should have put that idea in your head. Get some sleep tonight. And go back up to the telescope tomorrow."

"First I'm going to the exercise room," I told Rawling. "You have no idea how badly I want to get these legs ready to walk."

Rawling smiled. "Maybe not. But I can guess. Go exercise. Then sleep. It will help your body."

Sleep. That would be good. But I knew I wouldn't sleep much. The headaches would hit me like clockwork, just like every night since leaving Earth.

And the next one, I guessed, would be on me in about two hours.

CHAPTER 18

From Rawling's office, I wheeled toward the exercise area to spend time with the weights. Even in the reduced gravity of Mars, Rawling had said I'd only be able to move five-pound weights a total of one inch with the leg machine.

But for me, that was incredible.

My legs were responding to my brain's commands. In that aspect, the operation had been successful. Now I needed to add muscle to legs that had never had muscle before. And then—I finally dared hope for it—I could teach those legs to walk.

If it weren't for my killer headaches and the approach of the Manchurian fleet, I would have been bouncing around for joy 24 hours a day.

For now, I was only going to approach everything one day at a time, knowing the Manchurians wouldn't be here for a while. And that included my weight program.

Just as I rounded the corner to the exercise area, someone in a regular jumpsuit uniform stepped out. I barely glimpsed his face as he walked away and told myself it was just my imagination.

That was not Luke Daab. As if I were going to go running to Rawling again. But maybe someone in the exercise area could tell me who it was.

Except it was empty when I rolled into it.

I headed straight to the leg machine. On it was taped an envelope with my name. I opened it, puzzled.

> *Tyce,*
>
> *Those headaches can kill you if you don't take it easy and stop looking for me. You haven't felt the worst of it yet. Expect a sample of how bad it can get within the next minute.*

In the next minute?

Someone was controlling my headaches?

Then I realized something. The man who had just stepped out of the exercise area had been in a standard blue jumpsuit. Not exercise gear. Why else had he been here, except to leave this note? But how had he known I would be coming here right now?

And how was he controlling the head—

I heard a scream. Dimly knew it was mine. I fell out of my wheelchair, flailing my arms at the pain. This headache was much worse than anything I'd felt before.

Even death would be better than this agony, a part of my mind thought.

The pain continued and continued until it hurt so bad I couldn't even scream.

I waited for a blackout to give me mercy, but it didn't come.

And finally, when the headache stopped pinching my brain, I gasped for breath. My body was shaking and sweating.

I had to find that person. If only to beg him never to do that to me again.

CHAPTER 19

"Tyce?"

The voice came from outside the doorway of my bedroom. I was just about to roll out of my wheelchair and get into bed. After that headache attack, there was no way I could exercise. Half an hour had passed before I could even get back to our minidome. I was still trembling, and I'd thrown up twice from the aftereffects of the pain.

It was now 8:30 p.m. Mom and Dad had been so concerned about me that they'd gone to get Rawling.

"Yes, Rawling," I said. My voice was a croak. "Come in."

He did, carrying the lead-wrapped belt that he'd used to shield me during the X-ray process.

"Great," I groaned. "More medical work. Got some needles for painkillers? Those pills you gave me haven't done a thing."

"I think I know why."

I glanced at my watch. "Speak quickly. If it follows the schedule, the next headache is due in less than a minute."

That was the worst of it. Knowing and anticipating when the headaches would arrive. Like getting up in the morning and knowing you had a dentist appointment. Except this was like three or four dentist appointments a day. Without the freezing.

"I thought it was strange that there were no medical notes about the implant in your spine," Rawling said. "So I went to your father this afternoon just before he took the shuttle up. The communications link between Mars and Earth might be down, but he still has his Terrataker database."

I knew exactly what Rawling meant. I'd been surprised to find out on Earth that my dad had been working against the Terratakers for years. He and Rawling were special agents who'd trained together in New York, even before the Mars Project was launched. And Dad had a list of every person with a known or suspected link to the Terratakers.

"Sure enough," Rawling said. "Far, far down the list, I spotted the name of one of the doctors on your medical team. His background shows him listed as a potential supporter of the Terratakers."

"But why would a Terrataker be allowed to—?"

"The Terratakers have plenty of spies and connections in

the World United Federation. I imagine that someone some-where pulled a string."

"Rawling, the operation was successful."

"More successful than you think. I scanned your spinal X-ray into the computer and zoomed in. That implant—"

I interrupted him with a low scream. The headache had arrived. I clenched my teeth against the pain and made no more noise.

"Tyce! Is it always this bad?"

I groaned.

"You should have told someone earlier."

I groaned again.

Rawling rushed forward with the lead belt. He wrapped it around my belly, then slid it down so that it rested on my hips.

And the pain stopped!

"That better?" Rawling asked.

I found myself panting with relief.

"Thought so."

"What is it?" I asked, amazed at the peace and calm I felt.

"The implant has tiny, tiny pincers. The nerves to your spinal column have grown in and around the pincers. I think someone is squeezing those nerves whenever they want to put you in agony. Spinal nerves are funny. Even though they're pinched in your back, the pain can be anywhere in your body."

"And the lead belt?" I queried. "Not that I'm complain-ing . . ."

"Shields you from whatever signals that person is using to activate the implant from a remote source."

I lifted the belt slightly. The pain returned in full force.

I lowered the belt. The pain stopped.

"Rawling." I was still panting. "It's the kind of relief that comes when someone finally quits hitting your thumb with a hammer."

"You'll get some sleep?"

"Yes!"

"Good. In the morning, come talk to me."

He left. Or at least I think he did.

I was so exhausted from fighting the pain that I was asleep before he could shut the door on his way out.

CHAPTER 20

A dream woke me. When I rubbed my eyes, the thought was
still there.

Hunt the hunter.

I was still half asleep.

Hunt the hunter.

Why was I having that thought? Was my subconscious
trying to tell me something? I tried to recall the details of the
dream. . . .

I was swimming in the ocean. Luke Daab cast a lure
from his fishing rod. He hooked me below the spine and
began to reel me in. Except in my dream I grew bigger and
stronger and turned into a half shark. Instead of letting
Luke Daab reel me in like a helpless fish, I turned and swam
hard. He was pulled into the water, and I turned around and

opened my big shark mouth and was just about to chomp on his head—

Weird dream. I remembered I had woken up just as Luke screamed. With the same scream of pain that this implant had given me time after time over the last months.

I rubbed my eyes more.

Hunt the hunter.

I thought more about the dream. I realized that Luke had used the fishing rod to reel me in, but in the end, it became the weapon used on him.

Hunt the hunter.

When I realized what that meant, I tried to sit bolt upright.

It didn't work. I was still too weak, especially with the weight of the lead belt around my waist. I was only able to roll over and look at the clock. Eleven thirty at night. I'd slept nearly three hours straight, my longest stretch in months.

Hunt the hunter. Turn his weapon against him.

I was about to call out to Dad in our shared living area, but then I remembered. Dad had just left in the shuttle to pick up the rest of the cargo. Mom was most likely still in the lab.

But there was still plenty of time to find Rawling. He always tended to work late, so with luck, he'd still be in his office.

"Rawling!" I called out frantically.

It had been a struggle to get into my jumpsuit by myself, but at least with all the weight I'd lost in the body cast, my clothing was so loose it easily fit over the lead belt.

Rawling looked up from his desk as I rolled in. He had been writing on a pad of paper. "I expected you to sleep through the night."

"I think I know how to find him," I answered. "Use his weapon against him."

"Slow down. Him?"

"The person we think broke into the dome. The person I think is Luke Daab. Who put a virus in the computer software. Who stole the triggers we need to launch our defense system against the Manchurian invasion. That him. Let's use his weapon against him."

Rawling gave me a smile. "Again. Slow down. His weapon?"

"Whatever device he's been using to activate the implant in my spinal column."

Rawling set his pen down. "How do you know it's the same person?"

"I've had those headaches all through the journey here," I explained quickly.

Rawling scratched his head, looking dubious.

"Remote activation technology is great," I continued, trying to follow my own reasoning, "but the most range I've heard of is 10,000 miles. It couldn't be someone from Earth, then, or someone from Mars. It had to be someone traveling with the fleet. But everyone who was part of the fleet was cleared by security checks. So it has to be the one person who hitchhiked along and landed his own space shuttle. That person didn't go through security clearance; I can guarantee you that."

An image flashed through my mind. Of my robot going up to the man in the space suit. Of the man pulling his arm out of his space-suit sleeve.

"And, Rawling," I finished, "when this guy entered the dome, he reached inside his space suit. It had to be for the remote. He wanted a headache to shut me and my robot control down. That tells me he's very familiar with the situation around here."

Rawling spun around in his chair a few times. It was a habit he had when he was thinking. I'd learned not to interrupt.

"I'll give you this," he said slowly. "Your hitchhiker theory was right. Your dad just radioed me from orbit. The unmanned spaceship that was carrying the surface-to-space missile system has marks on the outer hull where a space shuttle docked. And a close inspection of the interior showed that someone had been living in it. Which explains how the triggers to the missile system were stolen before they even reached Mars."

"So you'll agree it's possible the same person was zapping the implant in my spinal cord."

"Say I do agree . . . ," he began.

"Then we track him," I said, "by scanning for whatever wave technology his remote uses. I'm guessing X-ray. That's what we use for robot control. Find the frequency that triggers my implant, and then we can follow the same frequency right to its source. He'll never know we're looking for him, right up to the second we get him."

Rawling spun in his chair some more. After a few minutes he stared at me, his jaw set. "It's going to hurt you."

"So will a Manchurian fleet that lands when we don't have missiles to scare them away."

"We'll do it then," Rawling said.

"No, you won't." It was a voice behind us.

I turned just in time to see a face I recognized. Luke Daab's.

He held a neuron gun pointed at Rawling's head. If set on stun, the voltage of just one neuron gun could cripple him with the pain of an electrical jolt through the nerve pathways of his body. Although it didn't do permanent damage, it would temporarily paralyze his muscles and render him unconscious. But if on a different setting . . . I'd never seen those results, and I didn't want to.

Without warning, Daab pulled the trigger.

Rawling screamed briefly, then fell straight back over his chair. He twitched once on the floor, then made no movement at all.

"Hello, Tyce," Luke said. "So glad we could finally get together again."

CHAPTER 21

Luke Daab shut the door to Rawling's office and locked it.
Keeping the neuron gun trained at my head, he moved to
Rawling's desk and ripped the computer wires loose. He did
the same with the phone line.

I was trapped.

"Just in case you had thoughts of trying to reach anyone
when I left," Daab said casually. "I have no intention of letting you stop me ever again."

He was still as redheaded, mousy, and skinny as ever.
The only change seemed to be that his beach-ball belly was
a bit larger.

I couldn't speak. Was Rawling unconscious . . . or dead?

"Cat got your tongue?" Daab asked with a slight, twisted

smile and that nervous laugh of his. He yanked off my wrist buzzer and then pulled a small device from his pocket. He dangled the device just out of my reach. "Or is it a headache?"

I groaned. I didn't want him to realize that the lead wrap was shielding me from his remote. "Why?" I said between clenched teeth. Although I didn't have a headache, I still felt enough anguish that I didn't have to act out any pain.

Luke moved around behind my wheelchair. He spoke to my back. "Why the implant? Or why am I here?"

My world tilted. He had lifted the handles of my wheelchair. He gave a violent jerk, and I tumbled helplessly forward. My elbows crashed into the floor. I groaned again and slowly rolled over.

Daab sat in my wheelchair, smiling down on me. "I'm here in this office because you and Rawling have suddenly become a danger. This is a little earlier than I had planned to set everything in motion, but fortunately all the pieces are in place."

I said nothing.

"Why am I here on Mars?" he asked. "Oh, you've already figured that out. To get the dome ready for my friends. You're going to be a big help to me, Tyce. I've always known you were smart, but listening in on your conversations with Rawling confirmed it for me."

His catlike smile widened. "Oh yes, the first thing I did once I got inside was plant a simple bug under Rawling's desk. I wanted to know what was happening. It was great entertainment, listening to how you came to your conclusions. I was amazed at how accurate they were. That only proves it was a good choice to enlist you for our side."

"Never help," I said between clenched teeth. I tried to rise.

Daab stood from the wheelchair and kicked me back onto the floor. I was surprised at how strong a skinny guy like him could be.

As he turned around, I quickly shifted the lead belt, lifting it slightly upward. I couldn't depend on him announcing when he shut off the pain activator. I didn't want him to find out I had a shield, or he'd take away my only protection.

Immediately pain flooded my head. This time my groan of agony was real.

Daab sat back in the wheelchair, smiled, and dangled the remote again. "So far, on a scale of 1 to 10, I've kept this down to 4. Today in the exercise room, I raised it to six. There's still a lot higher pain ahead for you. Unless you cooperate." He hit the remote. "Feel better now?"

The pain stopped. I let out a big sigh of relief.

"Perhaps you can concentrate now," Daab said. "So listen closely. Very soon, the only people living under the dome will be you, me, and all the other kids with robot-control capabilities. I know you are considered their leader. And you're going to make sure they continue assembling the generators so that everything is ready by the time Dr. Jordan and my other Terrataker and Manchurian friends arrive. If you don't help, the headaches will return—and you'll wish you were dead."

I remembered how bad it was in the exercise room, thinking that I would have begged to have the pain end.

"The fleet is two months away," I said. "I can't keep 50 kids from finding a way to stop you."

"I won't be in the dome." He sneered. "I'll be orbiting safely in space while I monitor the progress of the generator assembly. That's why you'll be in charge. And if you don't help, I'll shuttle back down once a week to execute kids until they finally get the message I'm serious."

Daab looked at his watch, as if it weren't a big deal to talk about killing people in cold blood. "Eleven forty-five. Good, all the robot-control kids should now be asleep in their nice little airtight, oxygen-filled dorm. When they wake up, they'll have the whole planet to themselves. Except, of course, for you and me."

Daab stood again, moved to the wall, and took down one of the two emergency oxygen tubes from beside a fire extinguisher. He dropped it on the floor in front of my face. "Ten minutes, give or take," he said. "Then it will do you a lot of good to wear this until the oxygen runs out."

He moved back to the wall and grabbed the other oxygen tube for himself. "I guess from your point of view it's a shame that Rawling didn't pay closer attention to those huge tanks labeled oxygen. You know, the ones that you thought were explosive devices?"

Daab kicked Rawling, who had not yet moved. Then Daab made himself comfortable again in my wheelchair. "I can give you the whole story later, of course, but here's the short of it. As you know, the upper levels of the World United Federation are riddled with Manchurian supporters. So it was very simple for them to arrange the emergency backup system. Seal the dorm. Add those oxygen tanks. No one questioned it. Only the tanks don't have oxygen. They hold a highly poisonous gas. The robot-control kids are safe, but all the adults will be dead as soon as I hook the tanks up to the ventilation system."

He glanced one more time at his watch. "Like I said, 10 minutes. Just before midnight. Make sure your oxygen mask is on. I'll have all the adults dead and the poisonous gas cleared before your supply runs out."

He began to roll the chair around me. "Nearly forgot." He looked down at me and giggled. "Can't leave you there on the floor to stop me now, can I?"

I didn't see his fingers activate the controls on the remote, but again a grenade went off in my brain. I screamed.

"That's a seven," he said harshly. "Enjoy it. I'll end your pain when I've released the gas. That will be your warning to put on your oxygen mask."

With that, he rolled to the door in my wheelchair, opened the door without rising, and cackled as he scooted out of Rawling's office.

CHAPTER 22

Ten minutes.

I could hardly move my arms, the pain was so intense. My fingers shook as I grabbed that lead belt. Twice my hands lost their grip. The third time, I managed to push it down and the shield blocked the transmission from the remote.

My head filled with blessed silence.

Ten minutes, I thought in agony.

I crawled to Rawling, dragging my oxygen tube. If he was alive, he was helpless, unable to protect himself.

I put my ear up to his mouth and heard breathing. I slipped the oxygen mask over his head and activated the tube. All of this had probably taken 30 seconds.

Now what?

Hunt the hunter.

The words of my dream came back with crystal clarity. Words that might save not only my life, but everyone's under the dome.

I was on the floor, close to the desk. Reaching up, I grabbed the edge of the desk and pulled myself off the floor. Leaning against the desk, I could stand.

Any other time, I would have shouted with joy. My legs, weak as they were, much as I needed the desk, still supported me! It truly was a miracle!

I shuffled around the desk to the closest wall. Keeping one hand on the desk, I reached to the wall with my other hand and pulled down a large, framed print of a sunset on Earth. I smashed the middle of it against the corner edge of the desk. Glass shattered. Now I had an empty frame.

Nine minutes.

I turned the frame on its side. The top of the frame was now waist-high to me. With the bottom of it against the floor, I held it beside me and leaned on it.

Then I took the first baby step of my life.

This was no time to celebrate. I was wobbly and felt like I would fall any second. But if I did, how could I get up without crawling back to the desk? And that would waste too many precious seconds.

The phrase of the dream came back to me again, making me feel stronger: *Hunt the hunter.*

I took the second baby step of my life. And the third. I tottered forward to the office door.

I was desperately hoping one thing. That Luke Daab had not risked raising any questions by being seen in my wheelchair. That he had jumped out almost as soon as he'd left the office.

I opened the door and peeked around the corner.

There it was. My wheelchair. I exhaled with relief.

I wanted to drop the heavy lead belt to be able to walk faster. But if I did, the headache pain would paralyze me. So I pushed ahead. It seemed I could hear every heartbeat as I made agonizingly slow progress.

Then, finally, I reached my wheelchair. I fell backward into it and dropped the picture frame that I had used as a cane.

Now I could move. I lifted my shield briefly. Pain zapped me, and I dropped the shield back into place. That told me Luke Daab hadn't yet released the gas.

I pictured him at the far end of the dome, hooking up the tanks of poisonous gas to the vent system.

I pictured the gas seeping into the air, an invisible killer, making this a dome of death.

I pictured Ashley and the other kids waking up in the morning, stepping outside their sealed dorm and finding all the bodies of the adults—Mom and Rawling among them.

I pictured Luke Daab forcing us to assemble the carbon-dioxide generators. The Manchurian fleet landing. And the Manchurians forcing all of us robot-control kids into slavery.

How much time did I have left to stop the release of the gas?

And what would I do about it? I wondered about rolling through the dome to yell out a warning. However, there were nearly 200 adults under the dome. Some were asleep. Some were working late or the night shift. No way would I be able to alert all of them, especially because Daab would hear me too. All he'd have to do was stun me with his neuron gun. In the confusion, he could slip away and return to the tanks of poisonous gas.

No, I'd have to stop Daab. But I was in a wheelchair. He was fully mobile and had a neuron gun.

Could Ashley help me? No, she was in the dorm. If I woke her and she opened the sealed entrance as the poisonous gas was released, all the kids would die too.

My thoughts spun wildly. What about somehow blocking the vents so that poison gas wouldn't reach anyone? Too many vents.

Wasn't there some way I could stop Luke Daab—and save the lives of all the people on Mars? Not to mention the future possibility of more people who would be able to make Mars their new home?

A minute later the solution hit me.

I turned my wheelchair and pushed hard toward the computer room.

The first thing I did was go to the wall and pull down an oxygen tube. I strapped it to my face. If I ran out of time, I didn't want my own body collapsing from the poisonous gas before I could accomplish my mission.

Second, I connected my spinal plug to a computer transmitter.

I guessed I was down to a minute.

I didn't waste time putting on a helmet. I'd keep my eyes closed and concentrate as much as possible. It was something I'd learned to do in emergencies.

The connection to my robot hit, and with it came that familiar sensation of falling, falling, falling. . . .

Earlier, Ashley and I had moved our robots back from the surface of Mars to just inside the dome.

When the robot's visual lenses opened, they showed her robot parked beside mine.

I directed the robot to shoot forward.

Now it had to be down to seconds before the gas released.

My robot whirred through the dome. I cornered and hit two techies who were walking slowly, deep in conversation. They bounced off the robot body.

"Hey! Hey!" they shouted in anger.

I kept going. I would apologize to them later. *If* I succeeded in saving their lives along with all the other adults under the dome.

My robot crashed through some plants as I took a shortcut. A scientist yelled at me.

I kept going.

Was it my imagination, or had a green cloud just been released through the vents?

Go, go, go! I shouted in my mind.

Then I reached it. The place in the dome Daab had punctured earlier. A repair was in place, of course.

Short of a welding torch, there was only one way to break through.

And I had it. The power of a six-foot-tall titanium robot moving at close to 30 miles an hour.

I raised the right arm of the robot and stretched it out horizontally in front of me. Like a spear. I made a fist. I sped up the robot's wheels. And aimed.

The arm of the robot pierced the repair patch at top speed. As the titanium broke through, the robot body slammed into the wall of the dome. As it fell backward, half destroyed, I yelled *Stop!* and severed the connection between the robot and my own brain waves.

Although the video lenses no longer sent information to

my brain, I didn't need the visuals of the robot to see if I had succeeded in puncturing the repair patch.

A great *whoosh* hit, as the atmosphere outside the dome began to suck out the air around me. It pulled a ribbon of green—the poisonous gas that had just started to settle downward toward the floor.

And best of all, the horns broke into full scream, sending an unmistakable warning to every person inside the dome to grab a nearby oxygen tube and strap it on.

All they would breathe until the poisonous gas cleared was life-giving oxygen.

CHAPTER 23

07.30.2043

Three months have passed since Luke Daab's last stand—since he almost made the Mars Dome a place of death. That night, not a single person died.

Except maybe Luke himself.

He fled during the confusion, breaking out of the dome in his space suit, running toward the space shuttle.

We knew that by the footprints we followed the next day.

By then the shuttle was gone.

Maybe he'd hoped to connect with Dr. Jordan,

the other Terratakers, and the Manchurian fleet. But only if his oxygen and water lasted.

If so, he hadn't planned on Rawling finding the surface-to-space missile triggers. Or the communications system software that Daab had hidden inside an empty oxygen tank.

So when the atomic weapons were ready and the news was broadcast to Earth, the Manchurian fleet simply turned around. Who could blame them? Even Terratakers and Manchurians weren't stupid. They knew when they couldn't win.

As for Luke Daab? If he had planned to meet them in the middle of space, he'd gambled wrong. Because of it, his space shuttle probably had become a tomb that would drift forever in space.

I stopped writing in my journal to think about that for a minute. The very thought made me shiver. I wasn't sure if even a guy like Luke Daab deserved that kind of an end.

Then I smiled and continued writing my update.

As for me, Rawling had determined that the implant wasn't going to harm my spinal nerves. At least not for years. By then, he'd said, an Earth ship would be able to bring in one of the mini-robots

capable of going into my bloodstream and working the nerves loose.

Was I walking yet?

Yes, slowly. But no one in the dome knew,
because I'd been practicing secretly.

And I had my own plan to show it when the
time was right.

Like tonight . . .

Midafternoon that day, the robots Ashley and I each controlled stood at the base of a great, gleaming copper globe,
fully five stories above the surface of the red planet. We
were surrounded by all the other robots controlled by the
other kids. Even so, with nearly 50 robots in formation
gathered at the base, the globe appeared overwhelmingly
large.

Behind us were the dome's platform buggies. As many
of the scientists and techies who could fit inside were staring
upward at the carbon-dioxide generator as well.

Five minutes earlier, the robots had been swarming two
half-assembled generators beside this one.

But the time had arrived—and nobody would be working
for the rest of the afternoon.

After the equipment had been put aside and the noise
from that died down, I could hear only the Martian wind—

and the sand it carried, which tapped against the robots' titanium shells.

Dying sunlight bounced off the copper. Already stars were visible above the darkening horizon.

"This is it, Tyce. History."

"I am glad you are with me, Ashley."

It just seemed right, to be out here in the robots. And it made room for other people to be in the platform buggies.

Among them were Mom, Dad, and Rawling. None of us wanted to miss this.

Back at the dome, the chief engineer was activating the first carbon-dioxide generator. A little wisp of white cloud left the top of the copper globe. It was surprisingly undramatic.

"That's it?" Ashley's robot said to mine. "How is that going to fill the atmosphere with—?"

Then a great mushroom of white rose higher and higher, growing wider and wider until it filled the sky above us. It would pour out this gas day after day, year after year, along with the five other generators that we'd been working so hard to assemble. And soon enough, the carbon dioxide—trapped by the thin Mars atmosphere that already existed—would begin to trap heat. It was a miracle—the way that it didn't just float off into space. Instead it stayed—and would enable plants to grow. Once plants could grow, they would produce oxygen. In the meantime, it was enough hope for Earth to keep countries from going to war.

"Yeah," I replied to her robot. "I guess that is it. Think it will work?"

The white cloud above us meant that millions of people currently on Earth would live. And in the centuries to come, millions and millions and millions more would survive—and thrive. It didn't mean all our problems on Mars—or the Earth's problems—were magically over. There were still years of work ahead—through developing new scientific theories that would lead to bigger, better technology; faster ways to move people between Earth and Mars; ways to help them adjust to a new world. But there was hope now for the future of humankind—enough hope to keep the peace. And all of us kids had had a lot to do with generating that hope. It was something we could be proud of.

Now some of the robot-control kids would choose to go back to Earth on the next spaceship, when Earth and Mars lined up in their closest orbits again. Others—like Ashley and me—could choose to stay. To make a place for ourselves and others in this exciting new world. A new world on a beautiful red planet.

Later, when the celebration at the dome quieted down, Ashley rolled me in my wheelchair to one of the garden spots. I'd asked her to take me there because of what I'd planned.

She stood beside my wheelchair, half covered with the shadows from the trees.

I rolled my wheelchair forward slightly to where I had hidden my comp-board, with its built-in DVD-gigarom player, beneath a bench.

I clicked a button. A quiet voice began to sing softly, with guitar as a background.

"What's this?" Ashley asked.

"An old ballad from Earth," I said. "About kids with hopes and dreams."

"I like it."

"Me too."

Then I stood up calmly . . . and walked toward Ashley.

"Tyce! You can . . . you can . . ." She wasn't able to finish as she began to cry with happiness for me.

"Yes, I can walk," I said.

I extended a hand. There had been something I'd been dreaming of doing for years. And I had practiced it over the last three months too. For hours with the song playing softly in my room.

"And there's something else I can do too." I smiled.

With a puzzled look on her face, Ashley took my hand.

"Care to dance?" I asked.

And so we did, with her tears falling freely on my shoulders.

SCIENCE AND GOD

You've probably noticed that the question of God's existence comes up in Robot Wars.

It's no accident, of course. I think this is one of the most important questions that we need to decide for ourselves. If God created the universe and there is more to life than what we can see, hear, taste, smell, or touch, that means we have to think of our own lives as more than just the time we spend on Earth.

On the other hand, if this universe was not created and God does not exist, then that might really change how you view your existence and how you live.

Sometimes science is presented in such a way that it suggests there is no God. To make any decision, it helps to know as much about the situation as possible. As you decide for yourself, I'd like to show in the Robot Wars series that many, many people—including famous scientists—don't see science this way.

As you might guess, I've spent a lot of time wondering about science and God, and I've spent a lot of time reading about what scientists have learned and concluded. Because of this, I wrote a nonfiction book called *Who Made The Moon?* and you can find information about it at www.whomadethemoon.com. If you ever read it, you'll see why science does not need to keep anyone away from God.

With that in mind, I've added a little bit more to this book—a couple of essays about the science in journals one and two of Robot Wars, based on what you can find in *Who Made The Moon?*

Sigmund Brouwer
www.whomadethemoon.com

JOURNAL ONE
IS DNA JUST ABOUT FINGERPRINTS?

Q: Is DNA just about fingerprints?

A: Your body comes with a complete set of instructions. This "master blueprint," called a *genome,* is what told your mother's body to make you into a human being instead of a frog or a dog or a cat. It's what makes you *you*, instead of your brother or sister. And you're still carrying that genome even as you grow up. It will never change.

A genome consists of *DNA* (you can think of DNA as the "building blocks of life") and associated protein molecules contained in something called *chromosomes.* The nucleus of each human cell contains two sets of chromosomes. One's from your dad. The other is from your mom.

The way it all works together is pretty complicated but

also very cool. And scientists are still trying to figure out how our bodies work. That's why the United States started the Human Genome Project in 1990—to figure out how to identify people's genes and map DNA. Currently it's being used to test babies for any genetic problems before they're born and to screen newborn babies. Mapping someone's DNA can even tell if someone is high-risk to develop cancer or confirm the diagnosis of a genetic disease. It can tell you how long you'll probably live. And it can even ID a criminal!

All of these are very good things, but there's also the risk of taking them too far. In Tyce's world of 2040, the Terratakers are arguing that everyone should be automatically tested, without having a say in it. And that means the DNA test results will have to be stored somewhere. That also means that those test results can fall into the wrong people's hands—people like Dr. Jordan, Luke Daab, and other Terratakers who want to identify skills, like those of the robot kids, that they can abuse.

It also means that suddenly those with "perfect" genes will become the highly prized people. Those with "imperfect" DNA—who have genetic defects or even those who aren't as "smart" as others—can become less important to the world. They can be considered "not fully human"—like the vice governor who seemed to imply that Tyce isn't as good as other humans because he's in a wheelchair. And that kind of thinking can lead to some scary things down the road. Like what happened to the Jews in concentration camps in the days of World War II and Hitler. They were considered a "nonhuman" race just because they were Jews.

So although these leaps ahead in science, like the Human Genome Project, can be good and can identify what's "unique" about you through your individual human genome, they can't and don't tell you what God does. He's the one who has made you with your particular, individual genes. That means in his eyes you're perfect—just as you are. No matter if your nose or teeth are crooked, you can't throw a baseball, or you can't run as fast as your sister. It also means that he has something special in mind for your life.

Just look at Tyce. Even though he's in a wheelchair, he was able to save the lives of millions of people at the Los Angeles nuclear plant. And because of his special skills, he figured out a unique way to rescue the robot kids near the Moon.

It all comes down to this. Your DNA and chromosomes—what makes your physical body—aren't what's most important. Instead, what makes you really human is that you've been created by God, implanted with a soul, and that only you, as a human, can have a relationship with God.

Your DNA isn't just about your fingerprints or your skills. It's actually God's fingerprint on you.

JOURNAL TWO
WHAT'S THE MATTER WITH MATTER?

Q: What's the matter with matter?

A: When matter and antimatter touch, *bam!* They explode, destroying each other. You see, matter is made up of what's called *quarks*; antimatter is made of *antiquarks*. Although quarks and antiquarks are identical to each other in most aspects, their touching and the subsequent explosion results in a burst of energy.

Physicists tell us that in the first moments of creation, the energy levels were so high that immediately upon self-destruction, new quarks and antiquarks were formed. But as the universe began to cool, there was no way for new quarks and antiquarks to replace the destroyed ones.

Basically all this technical stuff means that according to the laws of physics, nothing in this universe should exist.

And that means no Moon, no sun, no Mars, no Earth. And certainly no you.

Instead, for reasons physicists can't figure out, for every 10 billion antiquarks, the beginning universe created 10 billion and one quarks. And that one extra quark per every 10 billion antiquarks led to an infinite amount of matter that became the planets, stars, and galaxies of the universe.

Q: How is it that so much matter managed to survive? Why is there some matter rather than no matter?
A: Science cannot give us that answer. In fact, the chances that matter could survive are, according to a bigwig Oxford mathematician, Roger Penrose, less than one in 10123. That's a 10 followed by 123 zeros, which means the chances are not likely at all!

Yet somehow, against those kinds of odds, the universe grew in a way to make life possible on Earth. To make *your* life possible.

No matter what, many scientists argue that this shows us that the creation of the universe was not a random event. Our bodies are composed of the dust of the stars. The carbon and hydrogen and oxygen and trace elements are arranged in such a way that we can breathe, that our eyes can interpret light waves, and that our brains can generate thoughts and give instructions to our bodies (much as Tyce's brain waves tell the robot how to move in this story).

When you think about this, it's not so startling to think that the world was not only created, but it continues to spin and move at the direction of an invisible Creator. A Creator who exists beyond what we can see and sometimes sense physically. A Creator who sustains us through daily miracles. Like the fact that the sunlight is not too strong and not too weak. It comes from a star the perfect distance away from Earth in order to allow plants to grow in the dirt that was once stardust. Not only do our bodies depend on these plants, we find nutrition in the protein of animals that eat these plants.

The life cycle of all matter on this planet exists because of things like this—sunlight, water, and dirt—all possible because of the creation events set in motion by God at the beginning of time. It's that simple. And also that wonderful.

So in the end, science can't totally answer the question of "what's the matter with matter?"

But God can. And everything you learn about science will only strengthen the ability of your brain to accept his existence. Even when things seem impossible (like the reaction of matter and antimatter), God will always find a way.

ABOUT THE AUTHOR

Sigmund Brouwer, his wife, recording artist Cindy Morgan, and their daughters split living between Red Deer, Alberta, Canada, and Nashville, Tennessee. He has written several series of juvenile fiction and eight novels. Sigmund loves sports and plays golf and hockey. He also enjoys visiting schools to talk about books. He welcomes visitors to his Web site at www.coolreading.com.

The Wormling

From the minds of Jerry B. Jenkins and Chris Fabry comes a thrilling new action-packed fantasy that pits ultimate evil against ultimate good.

Book I
The Book of the King

Book II
The Sword of the Wormling

Book III
The Changeling

Book IV
The Minions of Time

Book V
The Author's Blood

All 5 books available now!

CP0138

Tim Carhardt is drifting through life with one goal—survival. Jamie Maxwell believes she can become—no, *will* become—the first female winner of the cup. But life isn't always as easy as it seems. What happens when dreams and faith hit the wall?

#1 *Blind Spot*
#2 *Over the Wall*
#3 *Overdrive*
#4 *Checkered Flag*

The four-book RPM series spans a year of the chase for the cup. Each story is filled with fast-paced races as well as fast-paced adventure off the track.

All four books available now!

CP0206